His Majesty's Hounds - Book 13

Sweet and Clean Regency Romance

Rescuing the Countess

Arietta Richmond

Dreamstone Publishing © 2018

www.dreamstonepublishing.com

Copyright © 2018 Dreamstone Publishing and Arietta Richmond

All rights reserved.

No parts of this work may be copied without the author's permission.

ISBN: 192549991X

ISBN-13: 978-1-925499-91-9

Disclaimer

This story is a work of fiction.

Names, characters, places, and incidents are the product of the author's imagination and are used fictitiously. Any resemblance to events, locales, or actual persons, living or dead, is entirely coincidental.

Some actual historical events and locations of the period may be referenced in passing.

Books by Arietta Richmond

His Majesty's Hounds

Claiming the Heart of a Duke

Intriguing the Viscount

Giving a Heart of Lace

Being Lady Harriet's Hero

Enchanting the Duke

Redeeming the Marquess

Finding the Duke's Heir

Winning the Merchant Earl

Healing Lord Barton

Kissing the Duke of Hearts

Loving the Bitter Baron

Falling for the Earl

Rescuing the Countess

Betting on a Lady's Heart (coming soon)

Attracting the Spymaster (coming soon)

Restoring the Earl's Honour (coming soon)

Other Books

The Scottish Governess (coming soon)

The Earl's Reluctant Fiancée (coming soon)

The Crew of the Seadragon's Soul Series,
(coming soon - a set of 10 linked novels)

A Duke's Daughters – The Elbury Bouquet
A Spinster for a Spy (Lily) (coming soon)
A Vixen for a Viscount (Hyacinth) (coming soon)
A Bluestocking for a Baron (Rose) (coming soon)
A Diamond for a Duke (Camellia) (coming soon)
A Minx for a Merchant (Primrose) (coming soon)
An Enchantress for an Earl (Violet) (coming soon)
A Maiden for a Marquess (Iris) (coming soon)
A Heart for an Heir (Thorne) (coming soon)

The Derbyshire Set
A Gift of Love (Prequel short story)
A Devil's Bargain (Prequel short story - coming soon)
The Earl's Unexpected Bride
The Captain's Compromised Heiress
The Viscount's Unsuitable Affair
The Derbyshire Set, Omnibus Edition, Volume 1
(contains the first three books in a single volume.)
The Count's Impetuous Seduction
The Rake's Unlikely Redemption
The Marquess' Scandalous Mistress
The Derbyshire Set, Omnibus Edition, Volume 2
(contains the second three books in a single volume.)
A Remembered Face (Bonus short story – coming soon)
The Marchioness' Second Chance (coming soon)
A Viscount's Reluctant Passion (coming soon)
Lady Theodora's Christmas Wish
The Duke's Improper Love (coming soon)

Dedication

For everyone who had the grace to be patient while this book, and every other book that I have written, was coming into existence, who provided cups of tea, and food, when the writing would not let me go, and endured countless times being asked for opinions.

For the readers who inspire me to continue writing, by buying my books! Especially for those of you who have taken the time to email me, or to leave reviews, and tell me what you love about these books, and what you'd like to see more of – thank you – I'm listening, I promise to write more about your favourite characters.

For my growing team of beta readers and advance reviewers – it's thanks to you that others can enjoy these books in the best presentation possible!

And for all the writers of Regency Historical Romance, whose books I read, who inspired me to write in this fascinating period.

Table of Contents

Dedication vii

Chapter One 1

Chapter Two 5

Chapter Three 11

Chapter Four 19

Chapter Five 31

Chapter Six 41

Chapter Seven 55

Chapter Eight 73

Chapter Nine 81

Chapter Ten 89

Chapter Eleven 99

Chapter Twelve 109

Chapter Thirteen	123
Chapter Fourteen	143
Chapter Fifteen	161
Chapter Sixteen	177
Epilogue	189
About the Author	192
Here is your preview of Betting on a Lady's Heart	194
Chapter One	195
Chapter Two	201
Books in the 'His Majesty's Hounds' Series	208
Books in 'The Derbyshire Set'	210
Regency Collections with Other Authors	212
Other Books from Dreamstone Publishing	214

ARIETTA RICHMOND

Chapter One

Charles Barrington, Viscount Wareham, watched as Lady Maria Loughbridge was wed to Lord Edmund Wollstonefort, the Earl of Granville. It was, they were saying, the wedding of the Season, even though it was the first wedding that Season. Maria looked beautiful, as always. He did not think it possible for her to look anything other than beautiful.

Once, when he had been younger, and foolish, he had looked at Maria, and thought that he would, one day, marry her. Then he had grown old enough to understand that the place of a third son in the world, even the third son of a Duke, was nothing – certainly not high enough for Viscount Chester to consider him as a suitor for his daughter. Nothing had ever been said – he had simply come to understand how the world worked. But he had never stopped seeing Maria as beautiful – beyond the surface beauty that everyone focused on.

He looked away, staring at the stone floor of the church, letting the words of the ceremony, binding her irrevocably to another man, wash over him.

He would find someone else to marry he was sure, for now that his father and Richard, his eldest brother, were dead and Hunter was Duke, he was no longer considering the church as a career. He did not, yet, really know what he would do. When the ceremony ended, he left the church with everyone else, and slipped through the crowd, into the streets. He would not attend the wedding breakfast – for he found little in the day to celebrate. For the first time since Martin's death three years before, drinking himself senseless in a tavern seemed like a good option.

~~~~~

"How dare you countermand my orders to my servants! You will not do so again, do you understand?"

Constance Wollstonefort, the Dowager Countess of Granville, spoke sharply, her tone scathing, as she glared at her daughter-in-law. Maria repressed a sigh, for that would only draw more of the woman's wrath, and looked sideways to her husband, hoping that he might defend her. He said nothing, as she had come to expect. She sadly acknowledged that he would never stand up to his mother.

"Yes, my Lady. I will endeavour to remember that instruction."

It was as close as she could go to rebellion. The woman would make her life miserable, no matter what she said. Whilst the first few months of her marriage had been pleasant, if less romantic than she had hoped, as soon as they had removed from London, to Myniard House, the Earl's estate in Wiltshire, things had changed for the worse.

Lady Granville had made it instantly obvious that no woman could ever have been good enough for her son, and that Maria fell far short of her standards in every way. Since then, Maria's life had been miserable. Her only relief was to go walking in the grounds of Myniard Park, spending as long away from the house as she could. The one advantage to her mother-in-law's attitude was that the woman expected nothing of her – in fact, she forbade Maria from having any influence in the household at all. Which left Maria with her time to herself, and no duties to fulfil, beyond those performed in her husband's bedchamber, on the occasions when he chose to call her there.

Some days, as she sat under the towering oak trees by the stream, she allowed herself to dream, to wonder what life would have been like, if she had married a different man. It was not that she disliked Edmund – he was kind, and genuinely cared for her. But he did not love her, and she did not love him. It was a cold kind of marriage, the exact opposite of the kind of thing that young girls dream of.

Her mother and father had been so happy when she had received the offer of marriage from Edmund. So proud of her, for marrying well. And she, good, obedient daughter that she had always been, had done as they said, and agreed to marry him. How foolishly innocent she had been.

She knew that dreaming now was pointless – she was married, and that was that. Perhaps, if she was lucky, Edmund would give her a child – with a child, she could spend all her love and energy there, and feel better in the world for it. But it had been months now, and she had not quickened, so, perhaps, it would not happen. The life that stretched before her seemed impossibly grey and miserable.

As always, as she returned from sitting by the stream, she collected herbs and medicinal plants, depositing them at the little gardener's cottage which she had claimed as her sanctuary, before going back to the house. At least that was one useful thing she could do. Tomorrow, she would hang them to dry, and consider what other plants she needed to gather before winter.

At dinner, she simply sat, watching her husband eat, finding her own appetite lacking. Edmund was a substantial man, whose hair was unfortunately thinning early, and there was no grace about him. Despite her determination not to think of 'might-have-beens', her mind would insist on comparing him to the young men she had known – her neighbours in childhood, the Barringtons, had three boys, all of whom had grown into fine looking men. If only Edmund looked more like that! She pushed aside the foolish wish, and forced herself to eat.

Lady Granville glared at her across the table, as if even her table manners were inadequate, and Maria wished herself invisible. There was not a day that passed when the woman did not find something about her to criticise. For Maria, who had been the golden child of her family, always beautiful, always praised, life at Myniard House had been the rudest awakening to the cruelty of the world possible.

In the end, she could not eat, and, pleading a megrim, took herself to her room. Once she had locked the door, like so many other nights, she cried herself to sleep.

Chapter Two

Edmund Wollstonefort, Earl of Granville, sat on his horse, staring at the building in front of him. It was far more rundown than he had expected. He sighed, an unpleasant, yet unavoidable thought coming to him.

It had to be intentional. Ever since his return to Myniard House with Maria, after their wedding, he had been seeing a side of his mother that he had never seen before. He had tried to ignore it, to deny the truth of what he saw, but he could no longer delude himself that way.

Since his father's death, his mother had been a never-failing support, giving him the strength to deal with his responsibilities as Earl, whilst he dealt with his grief, and then the rest of life. Once his grief was past, it had seemed reasonable to leave her to continue managing his estates, via Edwards, their rather long-suffering estate manager. He had seen no fault in anything that she had done, had never questioned her, as he never had throughout his childhood. But now... he had to face the fact that he may have been misguided in doing so.

For he could no longer deny the evidence of his own eyes and ears. His mother's treatment of Maria was harsh, and inappropriate. And his own failure to prevent that treatment was the biggest failure of his life. Which was why he was sitting here, today, staring at the dilapidated state of the Dower House.

It had once been beautiful. He remembered it, from when he had been a very small boy, and his grandmother had lived in it. It was well located, with an excellent view to the hills, and surrounded by what had once been a lovely garden. But the state of it now… the gardens were overrun with the wild growth of flowers and weeds that comes from years of neglect. The building itself had some broken windows, a collapsed section of roof, and at least one wall where the mortar was all but gone from between the stones.

It had to be intentional. His mother had ensured that every other building on his estates was in the best of repair, down to the last cow byre. For this to be as it was, there was only one possible explanation. She had specifically directed that it not be cared for.

And the logical conclusion to be drawn from that, was that she had done so to make it impossible for her to ever live there, to ensure that she remained in the main house, where she could continue to direct every aspect of his life. What had seemed an excellent arrangement to him, as a young man who cared more for hunting and drinking than for the tedium of estate management, no longer seemed so good. Now, as an older man, with a lovely new wife, the arrangement was constricting, embarrassing and painful. And all his own fault.

He sighed again, glaring at the building as if to make it magically repair itself.

Of course, nothing happened, except the small sound of a stone falling, as if the Dower House, to spite him, had chosen to crumble faster.

"Damn you! I will not allow it. I will repair the place, even if it means that I must learn far more of estate work than I ever wished to."

His voice echoed from the stones, and he felt foolish, talking to the old house, as if it could hear. But he had meant the words. He would see it repaired, and he would, somehow, find the courage, and the words, to cause his mother to move into it, to live. He would have some peace, a chance to make Maria happy, a chance to discover what he was, as a man, not as a child. It was both a frightening and a thrilling prospect.

He sat a little longer, considering how best to start, then, satisfied that he had at least the beginnings of a plan, he gathered up his reins, and turned the horse to ride across the wide expanse of his Park, and eventually back to Myniard House.

~~~~

"He's gone."

"Thank the Lord for that! My old knees be just about done in by all this crouching here."

"I thought we'd both be done in when you shifted and made that stone fall! What were you thinking man?"

"My knees – there's only so much pain a man can take!"

"Well – don't ever do that again. Suffer – it's better than risking our lives!"

"Now, now Jack, no need t'be nasty!"

"Nothin' nasty about it. Just the truth. Now, haul yerself up and let's get these boxes tucked away proper."

The two men rose from where they had crouched below a broken bay window of the Dower House, and moved across the faded glory of the parlour to a stack of crates which stood against one wall.

"Where d'ye think these should best go, Bob?"

"The cellar – s'nothin' in these what'll suffer from the damp down there."

"Right. Let's be about it."

They were silent a while, as they moved the crates from the parlour down into the deepest cellars, where they joined an impressive pile of other boxes, crates, chests, and an eclectic mix of other items. When the last one was moved, they stood, and went back up to the kitchens, where they had a stash of food laid by. They settled to eat.

"What about what his Lordship said, whilst he was sittin' there? What if he does start to fix this place up? What'll we do?"

"I don't rightly know. We need this place, and the old tower on silly old Lady Fremont's place. She's not a worry – only cares about the stars – doesn't notice what's under her own feet. But this place – all the goods we've got here won't fit in the tower cellars. And most of it needs to sit awhile before we can sell it, so's people forget about what we took."

"It'll have to be left as it is for now – surely he won't do anything fast. We need to be back down towards London two days from now, with the rest of the gang. There'll be rich pickings on the roads soon – some of the wealthy are already starting to leave London for the summer, even though its only spring – the ones who've already snagged husbands for their daughters, I'd expect. We won't be back here until we've got more that needs to be stored."

"But if he does do something?"

"Then we'll have to find a way to... discourage... him, maybe even incapacitate him for a while, until we can get it all moved somewhere else. I wouldn't worry though. He's never been one to bestir himself for anything much, except to hunt, and the Dowager wants nothin' to do with this place. So, it should be safe enough."

"True words, true words. We'll worry about it, if it happens, and not before."

~~~~~

Maria sat in the old gardener's cottage, sorting herbs, and tying them into bundles to hang to dry. Spring was wonderful, because it gave her much to do, as everything grew and flowered. Having something to do, which was useful, and required her to be out of the house for long periods of time, was a welcome relief, and soothed her. She dreaded the end of each day, when she had no choice but to return to Myniard House, clean the earth and pollen from her hands, and dress for dinner.

She dreamed of a day when the Dowager Countess would be elsewhere – anywhere, so long as she wasn't here. The idea of a time when she might actually be mistress of her own house, when the servants might dare to obey her, when her husband might care for her, and defend her, was like a child's fairy tale, so far was it from her daily life.

At least, when she was here, the servants treated her differently. Once they had discovered what she did, they had begun, very quietly, to bring her herbs and healing plants from their own gardens in the village or from the woodland paths. They came, also, to seek out tisanes and medicines for their families, which she was glad to provide to them.

It gave her hope for the future, to know that the servants regarded her well, that they only refused to obey in the House because of their fear of the Dowager Countess. She simply had to be something that she had never, ever, been good at – patient.

Chapter Three

Maria had learnt to be sure to be in the parlour at the time when mail might reasonably be expected to arrive. That way, if there were letters for her, she could get them from the footman, before the Dowager Countess knew they had arrived. In this small thing, the servants helped her, also waiting for moments when the Dowager was in another part of the house before placing the mail on the tray.

Weeks and weeks had gone by, with little change, and only a few letters – her mother was still very caught up with the Season, and Nerissa's unexpected success. Maria's life in Myniard House was a dreary round of painful dinners, and days spent avoiding her mother-in-law. Each time that she sat in the parlour, embroidering yet another useless item, she wanted desperately to be elsewhere, but she needed to be there at times other than when the mail arrived, if her subterfuge was to continue to be successful.

This day, however, was one when there was hope of mail. So, she sat, embroidering a rose on a handkerchief.

Her experience here had made her begin to understand Nerissa's dislike of pursuits which were 'officially ladylike' and to share her delight in escaping to the woods - dirt and grass stains notwithstanding.

There was a tap on the door. It opened carefully, and, when the footman was sure that she was alone, he stepped in, and, bowing, presented a letter. She took it, her heart beating a little faster at the thought of word from her family and friends. She tucked it into her embroidery basket, and calmly took herself up to her rooms, where she could lock the door, and guarantee herself some privacy to read it.

Once the door was locked, she settled into the chair beneath the window, both for better light to read, and to take advantage of the spring sunshine. Her hands shook a little as she broke the seal – it shocked her that she was reduced to this – where something as simple as her mother's ramblings in a letter were precious enough to set her shaking.

She read it through, shaking her head in disbelief at what she read, then read it again. Once she had finished, she allowed it to drop to her lap, unregarded, as a tumultuous cascade of emotions ran through her - joy, sadness, envy, bitterness, relief, and a sense of unreality.

Her sister, Nerissa, was to marry, and soon. She was to marry their neighbour, Hunter Barrington, Duke of Melton, improbable as that might have seemed only a few short weeks ago. Maria laughed, a shrill, self-mocking sound.

"Oh, dear sister, you do not know how lucky you are! To marry the man you have loved since you were ten years old! I only hope that he comes to love you."

Her words echoed in the empty room, and she heard the bitterness in her own voice. She sounded as harsh as the Dowager Countess. That fact horrified her, and brought her to silence.

She stared out the window, across the gardens and fields to the forested hills, acknowledging the beauty of this place that imprisoned her, and wore away at her soul. She envied her sister. And that thought made her laugh again. All her life, Maria had been the favoured child, and Nerissa the disregarded one, the hoyden who was ever in their mother's bad books. Now, somehow, Nerissa had changed, had bloomed into a beautiful woman, who was the toast of the Season. Maria sat here, married, and miserable, more disregarded and looked down upon every day than Nerissa ever had been. The irony of it all was not lost on her.

Only one thing stood out in that moment as worthy of relief, and of joy, apart from the fact that her sister would have a chance at true happiness - Nerissa's wedding was a chance to escape Myniard House, for a month, or maybe longer, if she was lucky. For her mother's letter asked that she and Edmund come to London as soon as possible, and stay as long as they might, to help with the preparations, attend the wedding, and spend some time with her family.

It was a request that Edmund could not, would not, refuse, and it was also one which did not include his mother, nor could it be twisted to do so. This evening, she would be happy to go down to dinner, for the first time since she had arrived in this house. For she could tell Edmund of it, in a situation where he could not avoid dealing with it, nor would he be able to refuse her.

~~~~~

Maria settled into her place at the dinner table, bringing as much grace as possible to her movements. She had actually bothered to dress her best, and was amused to see the irritated gleam in the Dowager's eyes, in response to Maria's composure. Edmund looked at her appreciatively, and she smiled at him, ignoring the Dowager's expression.

"Good evening."

"No better than any other."

The Dowager's voice was harsh, as usual.

"Err, yes, it is."

Edmund at least tried, caught between wishing to please both his mother and his wife. They dropped back into silence as the first course was served. Maria made herself eat, imagining it Nerissa's wedding breakfast, to blot out her actual surroundings. Once that course had been removed, she waited for her chance to speak, simply listening to the Dowager holding forth about the behaviour of people in the district.

"Really, some people have no sense of what is proper! Lady Fremont still insists on climbing that rickety stair on the old Norman tower in her grounds, to sit in the cold night air, staring at stars through that contraption of hers. It's a wonder she hasn't caught her death of cold. What kind of example is that, I ask you, for the young women of the district?"

"I don't know mother. She has always seemed rather harmless to me, if somewhat eccentric."

The Dowager sniffed, glaring at him down her nose.

"Just like a man! You should pay more attention to people. Take Lady Millicent, for example. You won't find a more delightful, biddable, and correct young lady anywhere. I still think you should have married her."

The Dowager glowered at Maria as she said this, her resentment of Maria's existence palpable. Edmund, miraculously, managed to raise the courage to answer her, and Maria had to force herself not to gape at him as he spoke.

"Now mother, let's not speak of that again. I didn't marry her. I married Maria, instead. And I am happy with that."

"Well I'm not! Useless, self-important, interfering piece that she is."

Maria's patience snapped, unwise as that might be.

"Lady Wollstonefort, I am right here. I do not appreciate your words. Surely it is your son's right to choose his own wife. And, regardless, what's done is done. We are married, for good or ill."

Her heart beat hard, and her palms became so damp that she laid her utensils down, for fear that she would drop them.

"For ill, if you ask me. And now I have to tolerate you, in my home. You'll drive me to an early grave!"

Whilst Maria, even if it was most unchristian of her, had a moment of considering that Lady Wollstonefort in an early grave might be better for everyone, she pushed that thought aside, and took the chance that the rest of the sentence had provided her.

"Actually, for a few months at least, you won't have to tolerate me in this house. I received a letter today. My sister is to marry in a short time, and my mother asks that Edmund and I come to London to assist and attend. It would be most inappropriate and ill-mannered if we did not go, wouldn't it, Edmund?"

Edmund looked at her, startled, as if she had somehow changed before his eyes. He shifted in his seat, uncomfortable under his mother's angry glare. Maria smiled at him, her heart in her throat, yet determined to succeed. He swallowed, hard, then nodded.

~~~~~

Edmund was almost ready to get the repairs to the Dower House under way. He had identified the best tradesman to do the work, and was now trying to decide what to have done first, having spent the day on that, he had been in a fairly good mood when he entered the dining room, and Maria's prettiness and careful appearance had added to that good mood.

A mood which had very rapidly been shattered by his mother. Now that he had admitted, to himself, that his mother was not perfect in everything, her failings were glaringly obvious. He wondered how he had spent so many years accepting them.

She was in fine form this evening, treating Maria as if she was simply not there, and being unpardonably rude to her. He had tried to divert his mother from her path of cruel comments, but had, as usual, failed. Then Maria had shocked him, utterly.

Not only had she just spoken against his mother, but she had just left him in a position where he had no choice but to agree to a trip to London, much to his mother's displeasure. He nodded.

"Err, it would. We must go, as your mother requests, Maria. A sister's wedding is no small thing. I will arrange it."

"Thank you, Edmund. Will we be able to leave the day after tomorrow? It is a long journey, and I wish to reach my family as soon as possible."

Edmund shifted in his seat, trapped. If they left that soon, the Dower House would have to wait, for he did not trust any of the servants here to carry out his requests, unless he was present to help them avoid his mother's wrath. Yet... it did appeal – not London, as such, he rather hated London – but a month or two, away from here, with Maria, and without his mother. Perhaps there was hope for their relationship, in London?

"Of course. I am certain that can be achieved."

Maria rewarded him with a bright smile, which reminded him of why he had been so taken with her to begin with, and his mother rewarded him with a glare which, had looks been daggers, would have seen him dead on the floor.

~~~~

"Thank you, Edmund."

Maria actually ate the rest of her dinner with enthusiasm, for the first time in weeks.

Even though the atmosphere in the room was icy, and everyone was uncomfortable, none of that mattered. All that mattered was that she would leave here in two days' time, and not be back for two months, at least.

~~~~~

That evening, as the dusk turned to dark, Lady Arabella Fremont climbed the rather precarious stairs of the old Norman tower on her property, to the rooftop area where her telescope waited. She shivered a little at the odd thumping noises from far below, but refused to let anything as insubstantial as a ghost stop her from studying the stars. Well, the stars, and the neighbourhood.

She turned the telescope to the neighbouring properties first. Most were boring, nothing happened but the gardeners and grooms moving about. But on the grounds of Myniard Park, things were more interesting. The crumbling building that was once a Dower House was haunted, she was sure of it. Dark shapes moved in and out of it, this night as many others. She could not see clearly, as the dusk deepened, but odd flickers of light lit its windows, and dark shapes moved in and out, from what looked like a cart – perhaps? Or was it just a shadow from the trees?

She shivered, glad that the more active ghosts were further away. At least the ones below her seemed to reserve their activity to simple thumps and bumps. Turning her telescope to the stars, she settled to more interesting viewing.

Chapter Four

London in Spring was beautiful, even with the smoke and dust – there were flowers everywhere, in gardens and window boxes, and in all of the parks. To Maria, that spring of 1816, it would have been beautiful regardless, because it was not Myniard House.

Wollstonefort House was better – for here she had spent those first few weeks of her marriage, when all had seemed well. She knew it, knew that the staff here would obey her, and that she could relax. She hoped that would be enough to improve things between her and Edmund. The thought of watching her sister marry happily, when her own marriage was still a mess, did not appeal.

She simply collapsed into the armchair in her bedroom, watching as her maid, Annie, unpacked her things. There were beautiful dresses that she might now wear – things that had never left the closet at Myniard House. Annie seemed happy, cheerfully humming a tune as she worked.

"Are you glad to be here Annie?"

"Oh yes, my Lady. I rather prefer London. The household here is... more relaxed... if you don't mind me saying."

"I don't mind at all. You're just telling the truth. At Myniard House, everyone is on edge, all the time."

"Yes, exactly, my Lady. Now, what would you like to wear for dinner? I'll get it ready, then come back to getting everything else set later."

"The rose gold gown, thank you. It makes the red in my hair stand out. Do you know, when I was a child, my hair was a strong auburn shade? But as I got older, it paled and the blonde took over – now you can barely see the red. My sister is lucky – Nerissa's hair has always been a light red shade, overlaid on dark gold, and has never changed. It wasn't popular years ago, but now, it seems, it's the height of fashion."

"Oh it is, it is my Lady. To have red gold hair that isn't orange is most sought after."

"It seems that my sister has had everything fall into place for her."

"I'm sure she'll be a beautiful bride, my Lady."

"Yes, I'm sure she will."

Maria closed her eyes and simply rested, while Annie went on with her work. The carriage had been with the Earls of Granville for a few generations – it was a beautiful piece of work, opulent and well fitted out, but, alas, it lacked the more modern type of springs, and was, at best, a rough ride, even on a good road. Her bones felt rattled out of place, and the comfortable chair was wonderful. She drifted into sleep.

~~~~~

The next day, Maria found herself swept up into a whirlwind. What started as a morning visit to her family at Chester House, became visits to the modiste, being dragged into a mass of planning of every aspect of the wedding, and being taken aside by everyone, individually, to be told each of their versions of the rather shocking way in which her sister had come to be betrothed to the Duke of Melton.

She wasn't sure what to think of it all – but she did find herself believing Nerissa's version of things, far more than anyone else's. Nerissa had never been prone to hiding things - well, apart from the books of Kevin's that she had stolen off with, to teach herself Latin. Nerissa was nervous, unsure if Hunter truly loved her, or was simply marrying her out of obligation. Maria genuinely hoped that he at least cared for Nerissa – she would not wish a marriage like her own on anyone!

It was most odd to see her sister the centre of attention, spoken to by everyone of consequence they met whilst out, and deferred to by many. It was as if their roles in life had been swapped. Maria now had much more sympathy for what Nerissa had gone through, whilst Maria had been the golden child.

By late afternoon, Nerissa had been deposited back at Chester House, exhausted by it all, but Maria was not allowed to rest – her mother demanded that she go with her to Barrington House, to consult with the Duchess, Hunter's mother.

Maria insisted on a short pause, and a small amount of food before they went. Her mother, it seemed, had far more stamina then she did. Whilst Maria sipped tea, there was a knock on the door – Hunter had arrived to take Nerissa for a drive in the park.

Nerissa, flushed, hurried into the room, her exhaustion forgotten. Maria watched with interest – there was no doubt that her sister loved this man now, even more than she had always loved him. And, Maria thought, Hunter loved Nerissa, even if he did not really know it yet. It was clear in the way that he looked at her, the way he took her hand to greet her.

Maria sighed, deeply envious. She was not sure that Edmund had ever looked at her quite like that. And Hunter was such a fine figure of a man! She remembered, yet again, the fact that Edmund had never cared greatly for his figure, although at least he was a fairly active man. Hunter and Nerissa departed for their drive in the park, barely aware of anyone else around them, and Lady Chester swept Maria up again.

"Time we were on our way. The Duchess is expecting us."

Soon, they were in a carriage again (blessedly, one with decent springs, given London's cobbled streets) on their way to Barrington House.

~~~~

Barrington House proved equally chaotic – Hunter's mother, who was a skilled organiser, but a little prone to dramatics, and Hunter's two sisters, greeted them with enthusiasm, and, after providing tea and biscuits, launched into the discussion of the wedding.

"Will our ballroom be big enough for the wedding breakfast? It would be terrible if we could not fit everyone in!"

"Mother, I am sure that it will all work out – if it's very crowded, you will have simply achieved a crush that any hostess might envy."

Hunter's sister Sybilla's voice held an edge of cynical amusement with the attitudes of the hostesses of the ton. The Duchess appeared to simply ignore the tone and focus on the words.

"Yes, I expect that you're right, Sybilla. Now. Do we have enough large marble urns to display all of the flowers we'll need, in the ballroom and elsewhere?"

"Of course we do Mother – they're stored in the attic, and in the back of the coach house – I arranged their storage after the last Ball you held here, before…"

Maria's mouth went dry at the sound of that voice. She knew it instantly – it had been ever present in her childhood, sometimes teasing her, but mostly talking to her brother Kevin. She turned slowly, and watched as Charles Barrington, Viscount Wareham, walked into the room.

Charles was three years younger than Hunter, and had once intended to go into the church. The death of both his father, and his eldest brother, whilst Hunter was still at war, had changed that. Now, he managed Hunter's estates for him, and was, until such time as Hunter might have a son, Hunter's heir to the dukedom.

The sun through the windows fell full upon him, drawing glints of deep red from the depths of his shining black hair.

His eyes met hers, and, for a moment, everything else fell away. There was something... unexpected... in his expression, something which left Maria feeling shaky and unsure. Then he pulled his eyes from hers, going to his mother and taking her hands in greeting.

"Charles! It's about time you arrived. Given that you know where the marble urns are, I will take that as you volunteering to arrange their disposition throughout the ballroom and the other rooms. I hope that you'll be here from now, until after the wedding – I'm sure that Hunter's estates can survive that long without your direct attention."

Charles laughed, and the warm, mellow tone of it shivered through Maria, vibrating deep inside her. She had known him for all of these years, but, somehow, today, she saw him differently – she saw the man that he had become, not the teasing boy that he had been. And the man was breath-taking. Confused, and a little embarrassed by her thoughts, she turned her attention aside, staring out the window. What was she doing, she, a married woman, thinking such thoughts about a man, no matter that he had been a friend since childhood?

"Yes Mother, I will be here until a little after the wedding. I've left instructions with our staff at each of the estates, to carry things through until then. You've no need to fear that I'll disappear on you, no matter how much I may be tempted to do so, as the wedding gets closer!"

The Duchess drew herself up and glared at him, as if affronted, then laughed herself, shaking her head.

"What have I done, to deserve children who are so unrepentantly impertinent?"

"Errrr, perhaps it is because you always encouraged us to think for ourselves?"

"Indeed, and perhaps I regret that now."

It was said with amusement, and love, not with any true annoyance, and Maria felt a sudden urge to tears, at the comparison between the Duchess' manner, and the Dowager Countess' manner, which had bedevilled her days for the last months. Nerissa was beyond lucky, in the situation that her marriage would bring her, no matter the unusual manner in which her betrothal had come about.

~~~~~

Charles had debated whether he should go and change, and brush the dust of travel from his clothes, before greeting the family, but had, in the end, been caught by the sound of his mother's voice from the parlour, and chosen to go and answer her question, before retiring to his rooms. The wedding to come was a delight and a trial for his mother, but he knew that she enjoyed every moment, even whilst she bemoaned the difficulties.

He spoke as he stepped through the door, his eyes, out of habit, scanning the room to see who, apart from his mother, was present. For a moment, everything stopped – he had no idea how long he stood there, between one step and the next, his eyes caught, his mind in shock. He should have expected it, but, somehow, he had not.

There, on the couch, sat Lady Maria... no, not Lady Maria any more, now she was the Countess of Granville.

He had not seen her since the day of her wedding, had not in fact, seen London since that day. When he had walked away from the church, after seeing her wed, he had gone to a tavern, and drunk himself almost senseless. It had not dulled the pain. He had returned to Barrington House, slept off the physical effects, and departed London the morning after. But the image of her in the church had never left him, nor the pain which came with it.

Now, her sister was to marry his brother – it was to be expected that he would see her – yet he had, it seemed, ignored that possibility. He could ignore it no longer, for she sat before him. Her head turned, the warm glow of the window behind her making her hair glow gold, with tiny glints of fire where the reddish strands caught the light, and her eyes met his. Time stopped.

Her eyes were full of something, something different – an echo of his own pain, almost? He was being unconscionably rude, staring. He forced himself to breathe, to drag his eyes away. She was married, she was not for him, never had been, no matter what his dreams. Time started again, laboured and painful, and he kept walking, going to greet his mother.

The short conversation restored him to his senses, and, once his mother let him turn away, he greeted the guests. Lady Chester was almost like an aunt, having known him since childhood, and seen the impact of all of the mischief that he had got up to, in collaboration with her son, Kevin.

"Good day to you, Lady Chester. I trust that you are enjoying all of this wedding preparation? Is a second wedding in the same year wonderful? Or is it all too much?"

Lady Chester laughed lightly at his question.

"Oh it's wonderful, if exhausting. A surprise, perhaps... but a good one."

He turned to Maria, suddenly uncertain, unsure what to say, and opted for simplicity.

"Lady Granville, delightful to see you again. I trust that marriage is treating you well?"

Something odd passed across her face, some trace of emotion that had nothing to do with happiness. It was fleeting, and gone, but left him wondering.

"Lord Wareham, I am indeed well, and glad to be here to see my sister wed – although I feel, at present, a little like I have been swept into a whirlwind, there is so much to arrange!"

Interesting – she had not, at all, really answered his question. Yet – she smiled, and he was not sure if he had imagined that moment of emotion – perhaps he had, for, no matter how much he wished she were not married, not bound to someone else, he wished her happy, more than anything. He would need to adjust to seeing her, for it seemed the next month would bring them into contact most days, as the wedding drew their families together.

He turned to his sisters, needing time to adjust, but her face was branded into his mind, in that tiny instant of unidentified emotion. He suspected that image would haunt him, until he understood what was behind her expression.

~~~~

The following weeks were a kind of sweet torture for Maria. She loved the time spent with her family, and tried, as much as she could, to make up for the fact that she had been so very self-centred before her marriage. She appreciated Nerissa's view of the world so much more, now – even if she could not tell Nerissa why. The continuing drabness of her marriage embarrassed her, in a way. She had been so proud of making a good match, so self-important about her new title. Yet now she thought such things irrelevant – love and happiness were of far greater value.

It had been a hard lesson to learn, but it had been learnt.

Each night, when she returned to Wollstonefort House, she hoped that Edmund would be glad to see her, that he might treat her as he had before their marriage. Yet he seemed unsure, a little withdrawn. They went to the theatre, and she enjoyed that, but it was as if he were a stranger – they did not talk of anything significant. And at night, whilst he occasionally came to her bed, it was no more positive an experience than it had been at Myniard House. She was puzzled, for she had heard some women whisper of 'the pleasures of the bedchamber' and had, before her marriage, been intrigued. It was all a rather large disappointment.

And, each day, when she saw Lord Wareham, the contrast between him and Edmund was impossible to ignore. Wareham was confident, bright, mostly cheerful, kind, and undoubtedly handsome. Edmund, simply, was not – he tried to be kind, but somehow seemed to completely miss what she cared about, or might desire. Life ahead of her looked very bleak – for if this time in London had not changed her relationship with her husband, perhaps nothing would. And once they returned to Myniard House... The thought was beyond depressing.

Still, each day, her worries about her husband were pushed aside by the wedding preparations. Mostly... she found herself looking forward to those moments when she saw Viscount Wareham (Charles, said her mental voice – no matter what title he wears now, he is still Charles, who played with me when I was a small child.). Their conversations were pragmatic – all to do with wedding organisation, yet, somehow, they made her feel better – until she got home, and faced, yet again, the fact that her husband did not make her feel good, even without the presence of his overbearing mother. And then she would feel guilty, all the pleasure of the day washed away in an instant.

~~~~

Finally, the day of the wedding had arrived. Charles was happy for his brother, for it had become obvious that Hunter did truly love Nerissa, and would be happy with her, yet he could not wait for the wedding to be done with. He needed to escape. Seeing Maria (for that was how he thought of her, no matter what title she bore now) almost every day, wore at him, like rough cloth scrubbed on the skin, and left him feeling sensitive to every tiny nuance of her emotions, her movements, her expressions.

It was a delight to be with her, and agony at the same time. For she was still Maria, still beautiful, perhaps more so, for she seemed to have grown as a person, to now be more concerned with the truth of a person than with appearances. Yet, the simple fact remained – she was married – beyond his reach forever. It left him feeling guilty, dirtied by his own thoughts, that he should desire her presence so much – yet he could not change that.

As he watched the ceremony, the soothing ritual of the marriage flowing over him, the age-old words spoken, echoing through the vaulted church, he was still acutely aware of Maria, just a short distance away. She watched her sister, watched the joy that was evident in both Nerissa and Hunter, with an odd little smile – almost wry – and her eyes glittered with unshed tears. He had the strangest feeling that they were not tears of happiness.

Again, the urge seized him – to discover what was hidden by her determined smiles, to uncover the secrets of those fleeting emotions that he saw in her face, when she thought no one observed her. He pushed it aside. It was not his place to care.

Soon, it was done, and the newlywed couple left the church, to much acclaim from all. Charles stood in the shadow of the church door, watching as they departed in the carriage, his mind lost, months in the past, when here, in this same church, he had watched Maria wed. The temptation to go and drink himself blind rose again. He pushed it aside – his brother expected him to be there, for the rest of the day, and he would be – no matter the pain it brought.

Chapter Five

Two hours later, Charles took his seat at the table reserved for the family, to eat. He discovered that he had been placed between his brother's new wife, and Maria. On Maria's other side sat her husband. He watched the man, and his interactions with Maria, with interest, which soon became amazement. The Earl of Granville had not been present at any of the wedding planning, so this was Charles' first chance to see him and Maria together. He had to conclude that the man was mad, or blind. For he sat there, ignoring his beautiful wife, instead utterly absorbed by a conversation about hunting with Charles' great uncle Alfred, who sat on the Earl's other side.

Nerissa was completely focussed on Hunter, and Charles, perforce, turned to Maria, unable to leave her sitting silent and disregarded.

"My Lady, I must ask – are you as glad as I am that our siblings are now wed? For, much as I hold my brother in high regard, the last few weeks have been exhausting."

She turned to him, her pale green eyes reflecting a moment's amusement, which slipped away, to be replaced by something that looked almost like sadness.

"I am, for I wish them every happiness in the world – they are so obviously right for each other - yet I am not, for this day's completion brings closer the time when I will leave all those dear to me, who are gathered here, and return to the country."

"You do not enjoy life in the country?" Her eyes flicked towards her husband a moment, then back to him. She sighed and looked down at her clasped hands before replying.

"The countryside is pleasant enough, and I must admit that Myniard Park is beautiful, yet..." Her voice trailed off, and she stared out across the room, as if not seeing what was in front of her at all. After a moment, she continued, her voice very soft, "...I do not always find the society available to me to be pleasant." Charles had the sense that she had just said more than she had intended, that he had been privileged to receive a confidence. He felt honoured – yet perhaps he was imagining it?

"Oh? I have always felt that we were lucky in our neighbours at Meltonbrook Chase – are you not so blessed at Myniard House?"

Her smile was brittle, strained, and she paused, as if considering her next words very carefully. He waited, wondering what was beneath her seemingly calm surface, that required such careful thought. Her eyes locked with his, and her words came slowly, freighted with what was unsaid.

"I would not say that it is the neighbours who are the issue, exactly."

That sentence could be taken so many ways – which did she mean? Did she refer to her husband? Surely not! And yet... here they sat, whilst the man ignored her. Or was there more to it than even that? The more he saw of her, the more he learned, the more curious Charles became. And the more certain that he had, indeed, seen flashes of sadness and pain in her eyes, always quickly hidden. She might be forever lost to him, yet he could not bear to see her suffer such pain as those last words implied.

"Ah, I see. Then it is somewhat more difficult to remedy than simply seeking out others to spend time with, from further afield?"

"Yes, that is a true assessment. And... even should I do that, I would not, as things are, invite others to visit my... home." The hesitation in her voice before that last word told him much that had not been said, and his heart broke for her. Here she sat, in a room filled with joy, as her sister went into what was obviously a love match, whilst she was ignored, and, it seemed, suffered some unspecified troubles at home. Troubles that he had no right to enquire into, nor any ability to resolve for her. What could he say?

"That sounds like an... unfortunate... position to be in. But surely there are things you can do, to fill your time? The running of a large household must at least provide distraction?" Her eyes snapped up to his, as if assessing the intent of his innocent words. He was caught by that look, frozen where he was. He suspected that, in that instant, despite his best intent, his feelings were clear on his face. Her expression changed, and a blush rose to her cheeks. Her eyes still clung to his, a moment more, full of a longing that he did not understand.

Then she turned her head away, and spoke in a whisper, as if to be sure that no one else heard.

"It would… were I permitted to do so."

The bitterness was evident in every syllable, so sharp it edged towards the sound of despair. Charles drew back a moment, shocked, feeling her words almost as a physical blow. What happened, in that house, to leave her in such a state, so disempowered?

Instinctively, he reached out, his hand closing over hers, where they lay in her lap, tightly clasped together. What he had intended as a gesture of comfort became, in that instant, far more. Heat flared where they touched, flashing through his whole body - she looked up at him, startled, and it was clear that she felt something also. Shocked, he pulled his hand back, breathing hard. But their eyes remained locked, and, without words, spoke of all the 'might-have-beens' that lay between them. He struggled to continue to breathe, to find words, to go on as if nothing had happened. Eventually, he managed to look away from her eyes, and to speak.

"You shock me with what that implies, yet… I do not find myself surprised. Is there any way to… improve the situation?"

A small, brittle, self-mocking laugh escaped her.

"Were there one, I would have applied it by now, a thousand times over. I am left with patience, which has never been a strength for me, and grim determination."

He looked at her, knowing that he was doomed, knowing that, no matter what their circumstances, this woman held his heart, as she had since he was a boy.

"My Lady, should there be a time when you need assistance... always, you may call upon me. I know that what I have just said is, by all of society's standards, inappropriate, yet I must make this offer – I could not bear for you to suffer, if there was a way in which I might alleviate that condition."

She tensed, the sound of her sharply indrawn breath distinct to him, and her eyes glittered, as if unshed tears waited there. The moment that their eyes met extended, as if time had stopped, and he treasured the feeling, the sense that subterfuge had been stripped away, and something honest declared between them.

"I... appreciate your intent, and I am honoured that you would make such an offer. I will hold those words close in my memory, even whilst I pray that I never need to call upon you."

He nodded. Somehow, there was nothing left to say. By unspoken mutual consent, they allowed silence to take them, each acutely aware of the other, yet proceeding to eat, and drink, to observe others in the room, and to go on as if nothing had changed.

Yet everything had. Everything.

~~~~~

Charles did not sleep well, the conversation with Maria replaying itself over and over in his dreams. He was beyond glad when the day was quiet, as everyone recovered from the wedding, and the exhausting weeks leading up to it. He could not, he thought, have faced seeing Maria again, so soon, now that he had this new insight into her life.

He could not understand why her husband, blessed with a beautiful and intelligent woman like Maria, treated her so – ignoring her in public and, it seemed, making, or allowing her life to be made a misery, in private. How could a man do such a thing?

He went back to his normal routine of focusing on the management of the estates, and planned to leave London for his normal circuit of the estates within a week after the wedding. That would honour his promise to his mother, to stay until after the wedding, and remove him from the risk of seeing the woman he could never have, as soon as possible. And, he reminded himself, he still had another promise, one now three years old, to honour, a promise made to a dying man, to find and protect his wife. But he had not found Marion yet, and wondered if he ever would.

The day before he was to leave, Maria and her family came to dinner at Barrington House, and his need to escape her proximity was reinforced – for their eyes met, and his world shuddered again, as a blush rose to her cheeks, and she looked away. He would not do this. He would not see her again, unless she called upon him, or some future emergency made it unavoidable – he would not act in a manner dishonourable, regardless of what his heart wished for.

When he departed London the following morning, he knew that he left his heart behind.

~~~~~

Charles' words, during the wedding breakfast, had lodged in Maria's heart and soul.

They were a gift beyond measure, even if she could never act on them. Somehow, they made it a little easier. Edmund was no different, paying her little attention, and seeming unsure, almost nervous in how he treated her, but she made herself be gracious, and tried to encourage him to spend more time with her. Things between them eased a little, but still, there was no joy in it, and she could not see that, upon their return to Myniard House, there would be any improvement in her life.

When she saw Charles, at dinner at Barrington House, she felt herself stumble, almost tripping on the rug beneath her feet as she entered the room. A blush rose to her cheeks as their eyes met, and the undeniable truth shone in his face for a second, before he replaced that expression with an ordinary smile of greeting. What was she doing? She was married – she had been foolish enough to listen to her mother, and marry for a 'good title' rather than for love. Now, too late, she understood her mistake. She would live with her choices, she would not disgrace herself, no matter what she wanted. But it hurt.

When he declared, during the evening's conversation, that he was leaving London in the morning, Maria breathed a sigh of relief, even as her heart shattered at the thought of not seeing him again. It was better that way.

The next few weeks passed far too fast, whilst Lady Chester took the chance of being in London, with Maria present, to take her about on social visits. Maria went gladly – any excuse to stay in London, any excuse to avoid Myniard House, and the Dowager Countess. But, every night, when she lay in her cold bed, whether Edmund had visited her there or not, and closed her eyes, what came to mind was Charles – his face, and his words.

It was impossible that anything would ever happen, yet simply knowing that he cared helped.

When Hunter and Nerissa returned from their wedding trip, Maria made sure to spend time with Nerissa – wanting to assure herself of her sister's happiness, and to take this last chance of being surrounded by family before she was drawn inexorably back to the nightmare of Myniard House.

One afternoon, as they sat in the warmth of Nerissa's small private parlour, the sun streaming through the large windows, Maria dared to ask her sister the question that had been preying on her mind.

"Nerissa… I must ask…" Maria blushed, suddenly finding it difficult to speak the words she needed.

"Yes? What must you ask, Maria?"

"Nerissa, now that you are wed… are you happy? Happy in everything, I mean, including… in the bedchamber?" Nerissa stared at her a moment, a little shocked that Maria had asked, and wondering why, then laughed at the furious blush that was colouring Maria's cheeks.

"Oh Maria, why are you looking so embarrassed? Don't married ladies speak of these things all the time? But, in answer to your question, yes, I am happy, oh so very happy! I had heard women whisper of 'the pleasures of the bedchamber' of course – haven't most young women heard things they shouldn't? But I did not realise… mmmm… just how pleasant those things can be! And the ways to… well – I obviously lacked in imagination, before. But, surely, you know what I mean, for you have had months to discover these things, haven't you. You might have warned me!"

Maria struggled to know what to say, for Nerissa's admission had shaken her deeply – there was, it seemed from her words, far more to the experience than her life with Edmund had provided. Again, she envied her sister. Finally, she found words – words that would allow her to speak, without admitting the depressing state of her own marriage.

"But talking to you about such things before you were married would have been highly improper!"

Nerissa laughed again, a sound full of joy and genuine shared amusement.

"Maria! You always were the good girl, always doing what society says is right, so I expect that I should have anticipated that answer. But I was always the one who did not care overmuch for propriety – and I think that a helpful conversation on the subject before marriage would have been ideal. Don't worry though, as you can tell, it has all worked out for the best. I am so, so happy with my life now – more than I ever imagined possible, just a few months ago. I hope that you are also happy, Maria?"

Maria took a deep breath. Lying was not something she liked to do, but she was about to do just that. She could not, in any way, disrupt Nerissa's happiness. And if she admitted that she was far from happy in her own marriage, then Nerissa would be distressed – for Nerissa always genuinely cared for those around her.

"Oh yes, I am happy. Living at Myniard House has given me a new appreciation for the woods and fields – I think that I now understand far better why you were always rushing off to roam the countryside when we were younger."

Nerissa looked at her a moment, and Maria prayed that, even if she saw through her deflection of the true question, she would be kind, and let it pass.

"Good, I would not like it if you were not happy. I must say, even when you used to go out and pick herbs and flowers, I never expected you to start liking the countryside – you were always so worried about getting your clothes and shoes dirty."

"Well, we can all change, can't we? Look at you – the toast of the Season, when mother always thought you too plain to be noticed. That's a rather dramatic change, isn't it?"

Nerissa laughed, shaking her head, and rang for tea.

"It is. I still don't quite believe it myself. I will never forget mother's face, that first day we went to Madame Beaumarais, and Madame told mother, directly, that she was blind, and could not see my potential. It was, I thought then, the best moment of my life."

The conversation flowed on, and Maria buried her sadness inside. She would think more on Nerissa's words later.

Chapter Six

As the carriage drew up before Myniard House, Maria shivered. Around her, the world was clothed in the rich gold tones of late summer, the flowers in full bloom, the crops ready to harvest, the sun high in the sky. Yet Myniard House itself seemed cold, ominous, looming over her like a threat. She turned to Edmund, who was smiling, oblivious to her unease.

"Are you glad to be back, Edmund?"

"I am, Maria – this is my home, far more so than the house in London. I look forward to some hunting, to riding across the Park and more. And I am sure that Mother will be delighted to see us."

Maria nodded, unable to speak her true thoughts, and searched for something suitable to say.

"Perhaps… we could invite some visitors? Your hunting friends? We could bring social activities to us?"

Edmund looked at her as if she had gone mad.

"Are you suggesting a house party? Mother would never allow it – the very thought of all of those people disrupting the peace of the house…"

He sounded truly scandalised at the idea. Maria's heart sank, and the very concept that this house contained any peace to disrupt brought the edge of a wry smile to her lips.

"Then perhaps you might host a hunt here, but everyone who attended could stay at the Inn? I am sure that you would enjoy the company hunting."

And, thought Maria, *I would find some way to spend time in the presence of those who came – simply to allow myself the sanity of converse with other people, outside those who live here!*

Edmund appeared to consider, then nodded.

"That might be acceptable. And you are right, I would enjoy company for a hunt, after these long weeks cramped up in London."

Their conversation was brought to an end as the footman opened the carriage door, lowered the steps, and stood ready to assist them out. As Maria stepped onto the gravel, she shuddered, feeling again the chill of the shadow of the house, which seemed to reach out, to pull her in, draining any warmth and happiness from her life. She forced the fanciful thought aside, and lifted her chin, walking into the cold marble foyer with a determined step.

She refused to be afraid, or to believe that there was no hope for her life – but maintaining that determination was difficult.

The butler greeted them, his expression neutral, as always – she wondered what he really thought about the world, but suspected that he would never reveal such a thing.

"My Lord, my Lady – The Dowager Countess has asked that you join her in the parlour before dinner. Your rooms have been aired and readied, so that you may refresh yourselves before that time."

"Thank you, Thompson."

Maria hurried towards the stairs, glad of the reprieve of a few hours before she must face the Dowager. As she did so, she heard the second carriage, bearing her maid, and Edmund's valet, draw up on the gravel. The relief of knowing that the one servant she actually trusted had arrived was great.

~~~~~

"Dressed like a London strumpet, I see. I should have expected you to comport yourself in such a disgraceful manner. It's all of a piece with the rest of you."

After the months in London, Maria had simply dressed as she would have for dinner, any evening at Wollstonefort House, or Chester House. She liked wearing beautiful clothes. She had not even considered how the Dowager would view it. She glanced at Edmund, but he appeared to either find his mother's words acceptable, or to be choosing not to react. For a moment, tears pricked her eyes, and she wished to run from the room.

She did not. This was her home, however much she loathed it, and she had to at least try to make her place here.

"This is, my Lady, a subdued and respectable example of current fashion. Chosen specifically because I could not bring myself to wear the more daring and immodest styles."

"I find that hard to countenance! Regardless, it is highly unsuitable for a respectable married woman. You dishonour my son by appearing a trollop. You will, from this point on, present yourself in a more appropriate fashion. Is that understood?"

The Dowager's tone was harsh, as always. Maria swallowed, repressing her rage, and her distress. Experience had taught her that direct conflict gained her nothing.

"As you wish, my Lady."

She settled onto the couch beside Edmund, who was behaving as if the conversation had not happened at all.

"So, mother, what has been happening here at Myniard whilst we have been trapped in the dreary confines of London?"

The Dowager glared at Maria before speaking.

"The harvests will be good – Edwards assures me that this year will, despite the colder than average summer, provide more profit than ever. The woods are well stocked with game, so your hunting will be good too. Other than that, little changes. The gossips in the town prattle on about every little thing – Lucy can never wait to tell me all of it, Lady Fremont is as eccentric as ever, maundering about the stars, the afterworld, hauntings and the like, and there have been some alarming incidents with highwaymen on the roads between here and London – you are lucky that you were not robbed!"

"Highwaymen? Surely not – none have been seen in this district for fifteen years or more."

"Highwaymen. The mail coach was robbed just two weeks ago, not twenty miles from here."

Edmund frowned, as if he struggled to believe such a thing still, yet he said nothing more about it.

"And have you kept in good health, Mother?"

"I have, no thanks to the slovenly no-goods that we employ. I have to continually hound them to keep the rooms warmed, to keep the drafts out of the house, to keep the bedding clean. If I just left it to them, we'd all take ill and die!"

Maria took a very deep breath – she expected her next words to be met with derision, but she had to try.

"Then… if it takes so much of your time to keep the household servants doing as they should, perhaps I could take that burden from you, and manage them, allowing you to focus on more important things?"

The Dowager glared at her, more ferociously than usual, and Edmund snapped his mouth closed, where he had gaped at the audacity of her words.

"I think not. What leads you to expect that I would trust a slattern like you to manage them? I'd more expect that you'd encourage their incompetence."

Maria said nothing. Edmund, as usual, did nothing to defend her. The months in London had changed nothing at all. Life looked bleak, and any appetite she might have had disappeared. She survived the remainder of the conversation by being silent, by appearing to agree with whatever bitter nastiness the Dowager spouted, whilst wearing an artificial smile. It was as if she had never been away.

Dinner was strained, and she barely ate, before retiring, claiming great tiredness from the travelling (which the Dowager dismissed as mawkish weakness), and, as so often before, cried herself to sleep.

~~~~

One night, not long after their return to Myniard House, when Edmund had actually come to her bed, Maria took the chance to speak to him, after he had been satisfied, hoping that the moment might make him more likely to listen.

"Edmund?"

"Yes, my dear?"

"I... I wanted to ask you something."

"Yes?"

"Do you... do you not think that your mother is somewhat overly harsh in her words to me? Surely, as your wife, it is my responsibility to take on the management of your household?"

Edmund looked at her, then looked away, as if very uncomfortable. When he spoke, he did not look back at her.

"Maria, I do understand that in most households, the wife would take on that responsibility. But, my mother has efficiently run this household and estate for thirty years. I see no reason to change something that works well. Her tone... can be somewhat overbearing, I know – but I am certain that she speaks with the best intent. I am not willing to take away from her the activities that she so efficiently carries out."

Maria sighed, and despite her intent, a tear escaped.

"Could you not even ask her to speak to me with a little more kindness? I am not a servant, after all – I am your wife. I know that I am not the one she wished you to marry, but surely, in deference to your choice…"

"No Maria, I will not argue with my mother. Nothing good would come of it."

Maria turned away, and buried her face in the pillow. There was, it seemed, no hope.

~~~~

Edmund hated himself, even as he spoke the words to Maria, which allowed him to avoid conflict with his mother. The time for that conflict would come, but not until the Dower House was ready. He did care for Maria, and now that he had become aware of his mother's failings, he flinched a little every time she spoke – yet he was not a brave man, not a strong man in many ways, he knew. He simply could not face daily arguments, until the time when he could hope to remove his mother from the house.

When Maria turned away from him, burying her face in the pillow, he was torn – part of him wanted to reach out to her, to hold and comfort her – but he was not certain that she would not, now, push him away. And, if he did comfort her, then surely she would expect him to do more, to challenge his mother.

In the end, he took the coward's path, and simply removed himself from the bed, and returned to his own room, gently closing the door as he left. Tomorrow, he would begin the work on the Dower House. The stonework first.

~~~~~

The following morning, after breaking his fast, Edmund set out to the Dower House. The stonemason he had summoned from the next town met him there, and stood in silence, staring at the state of the place.

"Can you repair it, make it liveable again?"

"It will take more than stonework to make this liveable, my Lord, but yes, I can repair the stonework. It is not so badly damaged."

"How long will it take, then?"

"Many weeks, my Lord – I'll need to take some walls apart and rebuild them – which in a building this size is a major effort. And I'll need to source suitable stone – this wasn't quarried near here – it will take time to get it."

"I had hoped for something faster… but, if that is what it takes, so be it. Proceed with the work. I will see you, here, once a week, to check on progress, and to pay you for the work done."

"As you wish, my Lord. And thank you for being considerate enough to pay as we go – too many Lords, if I may say so, never pay until everything is done, if they pay at all – which makes it hard for a man to feed his family."

Edmund waved aside his thanks. The important thing was to get the work underway, and to make sure that it continued, and the man was paid, without his mother hearing of it. He felt a pang at deceiving her, then hardened his heart.

The memory of Maria's distress gave him strength. By the time her birthday arrived, months in the future, and the London jeweller sent the piece he had commissioned for her, he fully intended his mother to be residing in the Dower house, and life to be very, very different.

~~~~

"Cor – did ye hear that!"

"I did, I did. He really is a goin' t' fix this place up. We'll have t' move everythin' to the cellars – if we leave it up here, that stonemason'll find it. And we'll have t' clear out all our things from the kitchen and everywhere. Maybe we can fit more in over at the old tower – if we convince that batty old Lady Fremont that it really is haunted..."

"That could be funny, but she's daft enough to believe it, so it's worth a try. We'll need to find a new hideyhole though, if'n we can."

They stayed hidden as the stonemason walked around the place, poking at the stone, muttering about the state of the walls, and finally, breathed a sigh of relief when he went away, still muttering, to start arranging the delivery of the necessary stone.

The next few weeks saw the Dower House a hive of activity, as the stolen goods stored in its rooms were removed – either into its deepest cellars, or to Lady Fremont's old Norman Tower, all carefully arranged so as not to coincide with the stonemason's visits, or reveal anything to him. Edmund saw no hint of what went on, beyond the stonemason's work.

~~~~~

Maria had taken to rising early – far earlier than the Dowager ever did – eating her breakfast in peace, then slipping from the house to her cottage, to the woods, to anywhere she could escape to. She had also been, bit by bit, searching through the fairly extensive library at Myniard House, which Edmund almost never used. It had proven a treasure trove.

Whenever she found anything useful, she carried it with her, at the next possible chance, so that her little cottage now boasted a growing shelf of books on all aspects of the science of healing. Today, she had discovered the best treasure yet – an ancient Herbal, most likely centuries old. She cradled it against her as she slipped from the house through the kitchen door.

The cook, and the kitchen maids, all studiously ignored her, looking away, so that, if asked, they could say that they had not seen her. She dearly wished that the servants would actively help her, but she understood their fear of the Dowager, and appreciated the small things they did for her.

The early sun was warm, even though the year was turning, and the view was breath-taking, where the colour of the trees was changing, painting the landscape in shades of gold, orange, and red. Once she was some distance from the house, she began to relax, and enjoy the walk.

If you had asked her, a year before, if she would ever enjoy simply being in the outdoors, she would have looked at you as if you were quite mad – now, she revelled in the simple peace of being away from the house.

Once at the cottage, she placed the Herbal with the other books, and considered what to do next with her day. With winter coming, she had been building up a stock of remedies for the sniffles and ills that came with the cold. Her stock of dried herbs was growing, as was the selection of bottled tinctures arrayed on her shelves.

On her work table, she found a pile of freshly picked plants, and a stack of small bottles. She had no idea who had left them for her – but once the servants and the farmers had come to realise what she did here, this happened regularly – people left her things that she needed. And, more and more, they came cautiously to the cottage, and asked her help with the ailments of their families. It pleased her – gave her purpose in her day.

She sent a prayer in thanks for the existence of the old Nanny who had care for her as a child, who had nurtured her interest in these things. Then, she had not cared for the outdoors, or the dirt and mess, but she had cared for the plants that it provided, and what could be done with them. Nerissa had not been the only one to steal off with Kevin's books and teach herself Latin.

The idea that something so simple as a plant, treated correctly, could cure the ailments which plagued people was endlessly fascinating – and had now become the thing that kept her from going completely mad. The time she had been in London had cost her considerably, in terms of the chance to build up her stock of plants – but the gifts of the common people had helped to balance that out.

Now, she set herself to work for the day, to forget, for a while, that Myniard House existed, or that her marriage was miserable.

~~~~~

The weeks passed, and Maria fell back into the miserable pattern of Myniard House – spending her days outdoors, wandering Myniard Park, or in the cottage, preparing simples, then enduring the evening of being criticised for anything and everything, before sleeping – cold and alone, most of the time.

Occasionally, the Dowager would invite someone of significance in the area to dinner, and expected Maria to perform, to her specification, as the quiet and obedient wife. For the sake of peace, Maria did so – but it left her angry, and ever more unhappy. She dreaded the coming winter, in some ways for, with the cold and snow, she would be less able to escape the house.

As November came to a close, the Dowager announced, one evening, that she had invited Lord and Lady Alderwood, and their daughter, Lady Millicent, to dinner the following day. Maria smiled and nodded, stood calmly whilst informed of how she would dress, and how she would behave, then, as usual retired early. The dinner would be unbearable – she knew that immediately, for Lady Millicent Stumbleford had been the Dowager's preference for becoming Edmund's wife.

She would cope. But it would be difficult. The day went by far too fast, and she returned to the house early to ready herself. As she washed the dirt and the dust of herbs from under her fingernails, she stopped a moment, staring at herself in the mirror – where had the acknowledged beauty gone? Where was the girl who had looked down on her sister's tomboy pursuits, and prided herself on her immaculate presentation?

That woman no longer existed. And, Maria thought, that was, for all the pain that had brought it about, a good thing – she thought that her understanding of the world was far better now. She shook the thoughts aside, and focused on her preparations.

Annie assisted her to dress – in the dress that the Dowager had dictated that she wear, and did her hair, as the Dowager had required – up, and looking tidy, but not overly elaborate. The end result was a plain woman, with little to recommend her but the elegant shape of her face, and the line of her neck, which no amount of dowdy dressing could disguise.

She sighed, thanked Annie for her efforts, and went downstairs, steeling herself for the inevitable discomfort of the evening. At least the Dowager would not outright disparage her to her face in front of guests.

In the parlour, the Dowager was waiting. Edmund sat in his preferred chair by the fire, but the Dowager stood, looking imperious, and glared at Maria, examining her carefully, obviously looking for something to criticise. Maria forced a smile to her face, and pretended that this was just another friendly social occasion, similar to those she had experienced in London.

"Good evening Lady Granville. I trust that your day went well?"

The Dowager twisted her lips for a moment, before deigning to answer.

"As well as can be expected, with all of the incompetents that I must deal with."

Her tone implied that Maria was included in that group.

At that moment, Maria was saved from the need to converse further by the sound of a knock on the door, soon followed by Thompson showing the guests into the room. The Dowager's whole demeanour changed, in an instant. A broad smile appeared on her face, and she went forward to greet the visitors.

"My dear Lord and Lady Alderwood, so nice to see you again! And Lady Millicent, you do look well. Come, please be seated, and partake of something to drink before dinner."

Lady Millicent, Maria thought, did not look well at all. As she always did, she looked pasty faced, a little frail and nervous, and as if she would fade into the background if she could. Her dress was three years out of date, and better suited to a younger girl than her. The girl almost never spoke in company, except to agree with something said to her. She did not speak now.

"So good to be here again, Lady Granville, so good – isn't it, my dear?"

It was unclear whether Lord Alderwood referred to his wife or daughter, but both nodded sycophantically at the question. The man's voice boomed, echoing in the room, and he seemed overly cheerful. Maria stepped forward beside Edmund, and greeted them in turn. Lord Alderwood's greeting to her was cold, barely polite – it had been ever so, since she had arrived here – he, like the Dowager, had always hoped that Edmund would marry his daughter.

Edmund simply looked embarrassed, as he always did with the Alderwoods – as she suspected his mother intended that he feel. The evening was long, and unpleasant for everyone, it seemed – everyone except the Dowager, and Lord Alderwood.

Chapter Seven

The air was cold as Maria walked along the lane that ran from near the home farm to the gatekeeper's cottage. With December had come the true chill of winter setting in, and her daily walks were far less pleasant now. Still, the basket on her arm contained quite a few plants that she would need for the winter's possets and tonics.

This lane was a place where certain plants grew, sheltered from the weather by the hedges along its side, and she walked here regularly. She bent to pick more plants, careful not to crush the leaves, and, when she stood again, she found herself observed.

"Good day to you, my Lady. I must assume that you are the new Lady Granville. Allow me to be impertinent enough to introduce myself." He bowed, with some elegance, smiling. "I am Lewis Maddox, your gatekeeper's son. As a child, your husband was my friend, although I am far beneath his station. I have been looking forward to meeting the woman who captured his heart."

Maria was somewhat startled, having rarely conversed with a man who had not been formally introduced to her. But then, this was not a circumstance with any similarity to the drawing rooms of society. She decided to be gracious, curious about this man who had known Edmund for so long.

"I see. Yes, I am Lady Granville. I have met your parents, but... I have not seen you before?"

"I am a soldier, my Lady, and was amongst the last to leave France after the war ended. I have remained in the military, as it seems a good career for me. I am here for some weeks to see my family, and then I will be gone again."

"I see. Well, I wish you well in your career. But I must be on my way now. Good day to you."

She turned, returning the way she had come, a little uncomfortable, for she had never had such a conversation before, with a man she had never met, and a commoner as well. She was glad that he simply bowed again and wished her good day, and did not pursue the conversation further. He was a good-looking man, and had obviously not been injured in the war, unlike so many other men. At least he had been polite.

It intrigued her to think that Edmund had had a commoner as a childhood friend – she could not imagine the Dowager approving, so perhaps they had been circumspect about it. Once she reached her cottage, and set to work dealing with the plants she had picked, the incident slid from her thoughts, disregarded as unimportant.

~~~~~

Edmund rode out to the Dower House, as he regularly did. The first serious snow of the year lay on the ground around him, and he worried that the work would have to stop until winter was done. His worries were proved valid when he reached the building.

"Good day to you my Lord. I believe that I've made enough progress for the old House to be safe and snug for the winter – I've boarded up the broken windows, and repaired enough of the stone that the walls are all whole. I even, as you suggested, got a thatcher to do some temporary repairs on the roof. It will be good until the spring – for, as I'm sure you expected, I can't keep working in the snow."

Edmund nodded, drawing out a heavy purse to pay the man for his work so far. Much as he hated the delay, he knew that it was inevitable – he could not expect the man to freeze himself to death, trying to work in snow, on icy stone.

"Yes, I did expect this – and I thank you for the work you've done – it's good progress, and I look forward to seeing it continue come spring." He held out the purse, which the man accepted with alacrity. "You'll find that contains what we agreed on, for the work so far, and an amount to pay the thatcher, plus a little extra for you, and your family, to enjoy the Christmas season."

"My thanks, my Lord. You are far more generous than most I have worked for."

The stonemason gathered up his tools, climbed onto his gig, and drove away as Edmund wandered around the Dower House, imagining what it would look like, when finally restored to its former state.

From the edge of the nearby woods, a man watched him, and nodded in satisfaction when Edmund finally swung onto his horse and spoke, as if to the house.

"I will see you fully restored yet, and my mother living here. However long it takes, it will be done."

Edmund's voice echoed in the icy stillness, accompanied only by the drip of melting snow as it fell from the tree branches. He turned the horse, and rode back towards Myniard House. He had much to do – a hunt was arranged for a few days hence, his last chance to enjoy an energetic ride about the countryside with others of like mind, before the winter closed in completely.

The watcher in the woods rubbed his hands together, and also turned away.

~~~~~

"It's all closed up 'til spring. T' stonemason's gone, and 'is lordship won't be back 'til then either. So we're good t' sneak ourselves in and use it f' storin' stuff agin, until t' end o' winter."

"Good. T' old tower's cellars are fit t' burstin'. We can start t' move things t'morra, 'less'n it snows."

The two men strode through the trees, returning to their horses, and rode off, well pleased with their day.

~~~~~

Maria walked down the lane again, carefully studying the hedges and the sheltered spots below them.

She was looking for any last plants which had survived the bite of the snow. This would be her last chance to walk here, and gather herbs, until the end of winter. The chill soaked into her, even through her warm clothes, and she decided to call in at the gatekeeper's cottage, just to take the chance to get warm a little, before returning to her cottage, and then to Myniard House.

The gatekeeper was older, and Fiona, his second wife, much younger than he. She was a pleasant enough woman, but prone to gossip and, Maria suspected, desirous of improving her social status at any opportunity. Her meeting on this lane, some days before, came back to her. The man she had met – Lewis, wasn't it? – must be the child of the gatekeeper's first wife, for he seemed far too old to be Fiona's child, though she might well have raised him from the age of ten or so.

As she approached the cottage, she saw Fiona in the garden, and went towards her.

"Good afternoon, Fiona."

The woman looked up, startled, then smiled broadly.

"Good afternoon, my Lady. Looks like you and I have the same idea – to get the last of the growing things gathered, before the snow shrivels them."

"Exactly. The cold has really begun for this year – not that it was very warm at all, even in summer!"

"It has, it has. But, I've finished this now. Come in out of the cold a bit." She paused, thinking, then went on, "Do you like cats, my Lady? For we've kittens in the shed here, if you'd like to see them, and it's warm in there."

"I do most definitely like cats – even if they shed on my clothes. There is just something about them, all warm and purring, that is hard to dislike."

"Then come and see."

Fiona led her to the shed that provided cover for their single cow, and storage for hay, and whatever else they needed to put aside. The space was dim, and Maria's eyes struggled to adjust after the glare off the snow outside. As she stood, appreciating the warmth, waiting for her eyes to adapt, a voice came to her.

"Well met again, my Lady. I would not have expected to see you here."

It was Lewis, the man she had met on the lane. He sounded amused, and far too familiar in manner for her liking.

"Oh, so you've met my stepson, my Lady? How did that happen?"

Maria sensed Fiona's interest sharpen at the faint hint of possible gossip, and huffed a breath in annoyance before speaking, choosing her words with care.

"We met by accident, last week, as I was walking along the lane near here, and exchanged no more than an introduction and a polite greeting."

"And very polite you are – far more so to a commoner than most noble ladies!"

His voice was still filled with amusement, and the implication that she had been inappropriately friendly. Maria did not like it at all. She turned from him, dismissively, focussing on the tangle of kittens in the hay which was piled against one wall.

The mother cat stood, and came to sniff at her, before returning to the kittens. Maria gathered her skirts and crouched down to reach out a gentle fingertip to stroke them. They mewled at her touch, clinging to her finger, and exploring her. So warm, so simple, lives so uncomplicated – would that her own life was so simple!

She had hoped that ignoring Lewis would silence him, but, instead, he stepped closer and spoke again.

"I wish that I had the ability that cats have, to make everyone like me, just by being there."

How was she to answer that? Fiona watched, absorbing every nuance of every word. Maria had to stop this, now.

"I doubt that any person could achieve the simple likeability of a cat. And how would society go on if they did? It would be most inappropriate. I dislike the idea completely."

He laughed at her words, and it reminded her just how long it had been since she had experienced a cheerful, bantering conversation with a friend. However inappropriate his manner, his obvious pleasure and interest in her company was flattering, after so long feeling alone, and being subject to the Dowager's disparagement. But she was a married woman – one who really should not be here, no matter that Fiona was here as well. With a last gentle stroke of the tiny kittens, she rose, gathered up her basket, and turned.

"My thanks for the warmth, and for showing me the kittens, but I must be on my way now – if I walk briskly, it will keep me warm on the way back. Good day to you both."

She turned, and left, glad to be away from them.

~~~~~

Edmund found himself riding out to the Dower House again, even though the work had stopped. It had become a habit, now, after so many weeks. Seeing the place was soothing, seeing that it had begun to be repaired gave him hope for the future, hope that he might, one day, have the life he had imagined with Maria.

Until then, he would not antagonise his mother, he would simply keep the peace, as much as was possible, and plan for the future. He sat on his horse, staring at the place, then slipped down to walk around, touching the repaired walls, studying the grounds, envisioning the finished result. He would, he decided, come here often, to keep his determination fresh, even while winter prevented work.

As he often did, he spoke to the building, as if it could hear.

"I'll be back, often. I will hold to my promise; the repairs will be done. Just coming and seeing this, often, will keep my resolve hard."

He strode around the corner of the house, and across the rutted remains of its gravel drive. He paused. Looking down, as the ground slipped beneath his boots. The snow was churned to dirty slush, mixed with the muddy earth where the gravel had worn thin. It was as if many feet, and perhaps even a cart had been here. he shook his head. It must still be the effects of the stonemason and his men, although they had left weeks ago. After all, no one else had reason to be here.

Still, he muttered to himself as he walked.

"Who could have been here? And why?"

~~~~~

The two men had frozen to stillness where they stood in the kitchen of the Dower house, at the first sound of the man outside. They peered carefully through the crack in the boards that covered the broken window, and were alarmed to see the Earl outside.

"I thought as you said 'e'd be gone until spring!"

One answered the other in an equally quiet whisper.

"'E was supposed t' be. S' what 'e said t' the stonemason."

"Well, looks like 'e's changed 'is mind. E's muttering about comin' here regular like."

They watched as he strode across the grass at the corner of the house and onto the drive. He stopped.

"What's 'e lookin' at?"

"The ground. That's bad."

And then they heard the Earl speak again, a whisper to himself, but loud enough to carry on the cold crisp air.

"Who could have been here? And why?"

They looked at each other and panic settled into their faces.

"'E knows! What if 'e goes a digging? What if 'e finds things?"

"We'll have t' make sure 'e don't, then. There'll be a way."

∿∿∿∿

"You know, of course, that Lewis is back for a while? I thought so. He's always been a charming boy, but now, after a few years away, well… He's even struck up a friendship with Lady Granville – the young one, I mean, not the Dowager."

"Oh? Do tell, how did that come about?"

Lucy Morton's voice was a touch sharp, and she leaned closer to Fiona, her face filled with avid interest.

"Oh," Fiona waved a hand dismissively, "They met out walking – along the lane, I believe. He was impertinent enough to introduce himself, and she was… gracious… enough to converse with him. She's far more willing to speak kindly to a commoner than most of the nobility… and… after all, he is very charming. And then she came by just a few days ago, to see the kittens… and it was obvious that they've struck up a friendship…"

She watched Lucy's face, and smiled at her expression. Fiona loved nothing more than to have a piece of gossip before her friend. What Lucy would make of it, she didn't know, but an association of her family with the Countess could only do Fiona's social standing good.

"I see. Isn't that a little… inappropriate? No matter how charming, he is rather excessively beneath her social status. I wouldn't have thought it. But then… She's never quite seemed a suitable match for the Earl. Not what I would have chosen at all. When I was caring for him, as a boy, I always imagined a woman far more suitable for him…."

Lucy was reminding Fiona of her own long-standing association with the Lord Granville and his family. She'd always behaved as if she were superior to everyone else in the village because of it.

"Well... I've always found her to be kind, and those simples she makes have helped Mary's children. I admit, it's not a very genteel activity for a lady, grubbing about with plants and the like, but I can forgive her that for the results. I expect I'll be seeing more of her in the near future..."

Lucy snorted, as if finding the idea highly unlikely. But the conversation had disturbed her, nonetheless. Perhaps...

"You may think whatever you like, Fiona, but time will tell, time will tell. Now, I need to be off about my day. I'm sure I'll see you again soon – do keep me informed if this ... friendship... progresses."

"I will, I will. Good day to you then."

Fiona picked up her basket, and set off to find others in the village to gossip with. Lucy watched her go, then turned the other way. She might have known that useless London piece her Edmund had married would be a true strumpet! But, until now, there had been no true evidence of it. Now, however... It was obviously time for her to visit her old employer, the Dowager Countess. As much as the Dowager allowed, Lucy had become her friend, almost, over the years. The poor woman had needed someone to talk to, after her husband had passed on, and Lucy had been a trusted part of the household for so many years...

Perhaps she ought to have a word with the Earl as well. Poor Edmund should know what his wife was doing behind his back!

∿∿∿∿

Thompson showed Lucy into the Dowager's private parlour. His face was expressionless, but his posture was tense – as if he suspected something was about to happen. *Well,* thought Lucy, *it was. Let the coward flinch all he liked, she would stand for the truth.*

The Dowager greeted her, formal as always, but her dark eyes glittering with interest – Lucy only ever came to see her if there was gossip to deliver.

"Good day Mrs Morton, what brings you to visit me today?"

Lucy curtseyed, then settled on the couch that the Dowager waved her to.

"I hesitated about coming, my dear Lady Granville, but, in the end, I knew that I had to tell you, much as it distresses me to do so."

"Oh? And what distressing things must you tell me? Do get to the point, Mrs Morton."

"Well... it's that disgraceful London piece that your son married. She's proven what a fast, shameless piece she is. She's no sense of the honour her husband is due, nor of the respect due her station, none at all! She's struck up a... 'friendship' with the gatekeeper's son! At least that's what the gatekeeper's wife called it. A gazetted flirt, that's what she is, and, I wouldn't be surprised if she's far more than that, far more!"

The Dowager eyed her coldly, saying nothing at first, but Lucy saw her fists clench where they lay in her lap.

"I see. And how did this 'friendship' come about?"

"They met, I am told, when 'out walking along the lane', whatever that means. Still, the shameless hussy does wander about the estate alone, so perhaps it's possible – but as to whether it was an accidental meeting... well..."

The Dowager's face had hardened, and a red flush of anger rose to her cheeks.

"I should have expected that it would come to this. She has, as you say, no sense of decency, honour, or position. She'd dress like a London fancy piece if I allowed it in this house. But this, this goes beyond the pale. She has overstepped herself thoroughly this time."

At that moment, before Lucy could do more than nod her agreement with the Dowager's words, there was a tap at the door, and the Earl entered.

"Who has overstepped themselves, Mother?"

Lucy sat back, watching, enjoying the drama that played out before her – rarely had her words created such an impact. The Dowager looked her son in the eye and spoke, her tone that of a woman who had just been proven right, again.

"That useless strumpet you chose to marry. I told you, from the start, that she was not the woman for you, that you should have married dear Millicent, but would you listen? No! and see what a mess it has put us in now! I don't know how I'll hold my head up in society any more, I really don't."

Edmund looked somewhat puzzled, and glanced at Lucy, then back to his mother, before speaking again.

"I see. Exactly what has she done?"

"She has proven herself a gazetted flirt, a fancy piece as bad as her taste in clothes would suggest, and allowed inappropriate advances from a commoner! She has cast your honour into disrepute by doing so! I have no choice but to confront her about this behaviour, and demand that she seclude herself in the house – we cannot risk her tarnishing the family honour further!"

The Earl swallowed, looking, Lucy thought, rather uncomfortable, then simply nodded. Well, so he should look uncomfortable. He had disappointed her, and his mother, and now the result of his inappropriate choice was his to bear. This day had vindicated her opinions, in every way. The Dowager rang the bell, and, when a footman appeared, asked him to request that Lady Granville join them immediately. Then she turned to Lucy.

"My dear Mrs Morton, I must thank you for bringing this terrible disgrace to my attention so promptly. But we mustn't take up any more of your valuable time, and you have no need to be witness to any more inappropriate behaviour, but do visit again soon." Lucy was, it seemed dismissed. She hid her disappointment, and departed gracefully, but could not resist a satisfied smirk at the younger Lady Granville as she passed her in the hallway.

~~~~

A strange woman was leaving the Dowager's private parlour as Maria approached it. A woman who looked at her and smiled – not in a nice way.

Maria drew herself up, and ignored the woman, even though she was feeling very shaky. Any summons from the Dowager boded ill, and she dreaded what might await her in that parlour. The room was always overheated, and was filled with a clutter of ill-assorted furniture and keepsakes. It grated on Maria, even when empty. When its owner was present, it became unbearable.

Taking a deep breath, she tapped on the door, and entered when bid to. The Dowager stood, glaring at her, with even more venom in her expression than usual. Edmund sat, off to one side, looking very uncomfortable, and as if he, too, wanted to be anywhere else but there at this moment.

"You wanted to see me, my Lady?"

"I never want to see you. But in this case, it is necessary for me to tolerate the experience, at least for a short while. It has come to my attention that you have disgraced yourself, have dishonoured your husband's name and have proven, for once and all, that you are nothing more than a gazetted flirt with no sense of her place in the world!"

Maria gasped, her eyes going to Edmund. He shifted in his seat, but looked away, unwilling to meet her eyes. So, there would be no support from her husband. By now, she expected nothing different.

"My Lady, I do not know what you speak of. In what way do you believe I have done these things?"

"Typical! You are so unaware of propriety and correct behaviour that you do not even recognise your own failings!"

"My failings?"

"Your failings. As you seem oblivious, let me detail them to you. You have no idea how to dress with propriety, you wander the grounds unaccompanied, and may meet any random passing person without appropriate supervision, you have no respect for your reputation, nor that of your husband, you go so far as to form... friendships... with young men of common blood – and I daresay more than 'friendship', given your fast and flirtatious nature! That you do this is so well known that it is common gossip amongst the townspeople. I am disgusted by the disregard with which you have brought our ancient name into disrepute!"

Maria's heart sank. She had not thought Fiona so unkind as to have made an innocent conversation into something far more, simply for the sake of gossip. But it seemed that she was, that she had. The Dowager glared at her, waiting for a response of some kind. There was nothing Maria could say – nothing which would be believed, nothing which would change the Dowager's opinion. She was doomed regardless. Still, she had to say something.

"I have never intended..."

The Dowager cut her off with a wave of her hand.

"Do not try to defend yourself – there is no defence for such behaviour. You will, from now on, until I choose to release you from this edict, not go outside this house. If I cannot trust you to comport yourself correctly in outside company, even that of commoners, then you shall not be exposed to such situations at all. You may not argue with my choice, you must simply obey. Is that clear."

Maria stood, aghast.

To never leave the house! What of her cottage, the herbs still drying, the tinctures she had not yet made, to help the servants and the villagers through winter ailments? Yet the Dowager was right, in one terrible way – she had no possibility of fighting the woman's edict, especially when Edmund sat by and let it happen. Her only hope might lie in convincing Edmund to speak to his mother for her – but that would take much persuasion – Edmund still seemed unable to see the truth of his mother's behaviour.

Still, she resolved to try. She bowed her head and did her best to look meek and accepting.

"Good, I can see that you are not going to argue. You may go. I will inform the staff of this restriction, to ensure that they do not assist you in any foolish notion you may have, of leaving the house regardless."

Maria fought back tears – she was to be so humiliated that the staff were to be engaged as her jailors. She turned, and left the room. She did not allow the tears to fall until she was safely in her rooms, with the door locked.

~~~~

"No milord, there's no woman fits that description hereabouts. The only one that age lives with her mother, has a little boy. No idea about the father, she's likely a widow – the war took so many men."

"Thank you for the information, Innkeep. I'll have a meal of your excellent pie, and a tankard of ale before I get back on the road, if you would."

The Innkeeper nodded, and scurried off to bring the food.

Another possibility gone. When Martin had charged him with Marion's care, with his dying breath, Charles had never expected that request to lead to a years' long search for a missing woman. A woman who seemed to have simply disappeared, like the morning mist does in the light of the sun.

Three years later, he seemed no closer to finding her, and the failure ate at his self-respect. He would continue his rounds of Hunter's estates, and continue checking, and asking everywhere - surely, one day, he would find some hint of where she had gone.

His thoughts drifted in another direction entirely, as he slowly ate the pie. Maria. He wondered how her life went on, if she was any happier than she had been, at the time of Hunter and Nerissa's wedding. She was never far from his thoughts for long. He had, he knew, been avoiding going home to Meltonbrook Chase, for the proximity of Maria's childhood home, and everything around it reminded him, over and over, what he had lost, had never had a chance to reach for.

He would, to appease his mother, go home for Christmas Day – but he would not stay long, not even until twelfth night – he could not bear it. He would make an excuse, and return here, to Springhurst Chase, or maybe further north, to Moorwood Park. There were always estate matters to deal with. At least there, whilst he would still think of Maria, he would not be surrounded by tiny reminders every day.

Chapter Eight

Maria's hope of talking to Edmund was in vain. For the next few days, he avoided her, caught up in the arrangements for the hunt he was to host in a few days' time. She held herself with dignity, as much as she could, and those of the servants who had always been kind to her, as much as they could without incurring the Dowager's wrath, made sure that she knew of their unhappiness with the Dowager's edict. They did it in small ways – a little extra treat on her breakfast tray, greater attention to keeping her chambers warm, despite the snow which fell some days outside, and more.

Maria was grateful, but worried about her cottage and supplies. Eventually, she sent Annie to discreetly call upon the midwife, and let her know that she might go to the cottage and use any of the supplies she needed. Far better that things were used, than that they moulder away whilst Maria could not do anything about them.

When the day of the hunt arrived, Maria watched from her window as the men set off.

As always, Edmund sat his horse well, and looked more alive, more sure of himself, than he ever did in any other circumstance. If only he could find it in himself to be that certain when dealing with his mother, if only he were capable of seeing the world differently... she turned away, back into the warm room, no longer able to bear watching the men ride away, free to go where they wished, whilst she sat, imprisoned, with no hope of any improvement in her life.

Her thoughts went back to Nerissa's wedding, to the joy that her sister had found with Hunter, and to that conversation with Charles, at the wedding breakfast. It had not been wise of her to reveal to him her unhappiness, and yet... his words stayed with her, his offer of unconditional help should she need it had become a treasure that she clung to. No matter that she could not conceive of a situation in which she could call on him, without destroying both of their reputations irrevocably. Not that, between the efforts of the gossiping villagers, and the Dowager, she had much reputation left to ruin!

~~~~~

Three hours later, Maria was roused from her reading by a great outcry downstairs. She looked out the window to see the hunters returned, apparently in disarray. Curious, she left her rooms and descended the stairs. As she reached the bottom step, the front doors opened, and four men entered, carrying another man on a makeshift hurdle. It was Edmund.

Maria rushed forward, shocked, and afraid. Edmund was unconscious, his face a stark white. Blood marred his complexion, trickling from a gash at his hairline.

His clothes were soaking wet, and his body shook with shivers.

At that instant, the Dowager entered the hall, already speaking.

"What is the meaning of this immoderate noise? How dare you disrupt..."

Her face paled and her words trailed off as she saw Edmund, and she staggered a little, clutching a hall table for support. A groom stepped forward, twisting his cap between his hands in anguish, glancing between Maria and the Dowager, as if unsure who to address. In the end he lowered his eyes, and stared at the floor as he spoke.

"My Lady, it were terrible. The fox crossed the Stonefort River, jumping across the stones. The horses couldn't cross there, so's we went around to the old stone bridge, agoing as fast as you like, so's he didn't get away, so's we didn't lose the hounds. The bridge was slippery with ice from last night's snow, and the horses were slidin' about. Then, all of a sudden, his Lordship's horse twisted and bucked like I's never seen him do before, and his Lordship was flung from the saddle. He clipped his head right hard on the stone of the bridge, and dropped, all limp like, into the river. We pulled him out right quick, m'Lady, but that water's icy at this time o' year..."

Thompson, who had arrived in response to the commotion, stood next to the footman who had opened the door.

"Shall I send for the physician, my Lady?"

"Yes."

"Yes."

Maria and the Dowager spoke in the same instant, and stopped, glaring at each other. Maria would not back down – she would have a say in the care of her husband - she only hoped that the Dowager would not choose to argue. But it seemed that, for now, they were in accord. Maria dared to give an order.

"Carry him to his rooms, at once, and summon Potter immediately – we must get him out of those wet clothes, and keep him warm."

When the Dowager said nothing, the footman set off to find Potter, Edmund's valet, and the men lifted the hurdle and started, carefully, up the stairs. The Dowager watched them go, her face still grey with shock. Maria ignored her and followed the men up the stairs.

~~~~

The physician stepped into the parlour, where Maria and the Dowager waited, ignoring each other steadfastly.

"He's sleeping now, and I've left a draught with his valet to help with pain if he needs it. The cut will heal, but I can't know if the knock to his head has done more damage, inside. For now, the biggest concern is that he will take a chill to the lungs, and they'll fester. If that happens, it could turn to consumption. Keep him warm, and pray. If it does turn for the worse, I may need to bleed him, to draw out the bad humours from the river water."

Maria simply nodded, but inside she vowed that she would not allow the doctor to bleed Edmund, no matter what happened.

Everything she'd learned from her old nurse suggested that bleeding a patient simply hastened death.

The Dowager was still pale, and had taken the unprecedented step of asking for a brandy. The glass shook in her hand as she lowered it to the table beside her.

"Thank you. I will send for you if his condition worsens."

The physician bowed.

"Good day my Lady."

He barely nodded in Maria's direction, even though he had given the Dowager a full bow. Maria sighed – this was, it seemed, her life from now on – to be disregarded, and barely tolerated. She would not allow it to overwhelm her. Now, at least, she had purpose – she needed to keep Edmund alive. The thought of her life, if he died, was simply unbearable – for she was certain that the Dowager would find a way to blame her.

~~~~

"It's done. He won't be a worryin' us for the rest of winter, I'd say, after that. He'll likely be laid up in bed."

"True, but… are ye sure that was wise? I know, as we needed t' stop him from a'comin' here, but… are ye sure he'll live?"

"A'course he'll live. Those toffs can afford the best physicians an all. Now stop fussin' and let's get all this stuff moved into the old house afore someone sees the cart."

~~~~

Three weeks later, Christmas had come and gone, with Maria hardly noticing. Edmund had taken an infection in the lungs, despite all of their efforts to prevent it, and weakened by the day. Maria had tried to help with some of her simples, sending Annie to retrieve things from the cottage, but, whilst they eased his breathing for a while, nothing seemed to truly help.

She sat in the chair by his bed, listening to his laboured breathing, and fear filled her. She did not love him, that was true, but she had cared about him, as a person, even through the pain of realising that he would never defend her against his mother. She did not want him to die, but she was terribly afraid that he was going to.

The cut on his head was not truly healed either, although it was better, the infection there finally gone, but his lungs… that was a different matter. He rarely woke to true awareness, tossing and turning, struggling to breath, alternately searing hot and feeling like ice to the touch. The physician had insisted on bleeding him, and despite her objections, had done so, with the Dowager's support. It had been obvious, immediately, how much the bleeding had weakened him.

All she could do was keep trying, keep caring for him, so she did.

Another week passed, twelfth night was gone, and still he grew weaker. Exhausted after a long day, trying to fix what, it seemed, could not be fixed, Maria took herself to her bed. Potter would sit with him through the night. When she cried herself to sleep, this time, the tears were as much for Edmund as herself – even, in a way, for the Dowager, who was so distraught at her son's condition.

It felt as if barely a minute had passed when Annie shook her awake again.

"My Lady, I'm so sorry to wake you, but... it's his Lordship – he's gone! Potter says he just simply stopped breathing, a few minutes ago."

Maria shook the fog of sleep from her brain, slowly taking in what Annie had said.

"Gone? I... I had so hoped that we might save him... I..."

Tears came then, tears of grief for a life snuffed out before its time, and for everything that this would mean, to her, and to those around her. She allowed herself only a few moments before she wiped her eyes and pushed those feelings aside. There would be much to be done. Annie helped her dress, and she stepped out into the hallway, moving to Edmund's door.

In the room, Potter stood, his face showing his uncertainty. The Dowager stood there also, staring down at her unbreathing son. She looked, in that moment, smaller, older, weaker, than ever before. Then she heard the sound of Maria's steps, and spun towards her. The Dowager's face flushed, and contorted in grief fuelled anger.

"You! It is all your fault! I wish he had never set eyes on you! And your potions... I am sure that they made him worse, no doubt with intent. You never respected him, never behaved as you should. Well, I'll make sure you have nothing from this, nothing, do you hear me?"

Maria gaped at her for a moment, reeling from the force of the attack. What could she possibly say? She cared nothing for what she might inherit, would never have cared about that.

The accusations, after the last few weeks where she had put everything she had into trying to save Edmund, cut deep. Tears rose in her eyes.

"He was my husband! I care nothing for inheritance – I wanted him to live, I did my best…."

"I do not believe you! You're a faithless interfering strumpet. I'll make you regret the day you stepped foot in this house. Get out of my sight, leave me to farewell my son in private!"

Maria looked towards the still form on the bed, and said her goodbyes silently, then turned, with as much dignity as possible, and left the room.

Chapter Nine

The vicar's voice droned on, as he spoke the final words of Edmund's funeral rites. Maria felt dazed, still struggling to believe that Edmund was gone. She had not thought past this moment, and life beyond now seemed undefined, impossible to imagine.

At least she had family around her. Her parents, her brother, Nerissa and Hunter, and Charles... they all sat close to her on the worn pews of the old stone church. The Dowager, heavily veiled in the deepest stark black, had chosen to sit on the other side of the church, and was accompanied by an old woman that Maria had once seen before – in the hallway of Myniard House, just before that terrible conversation in which she had been confined to the house. Who was she? Maria considered it, vaguely, before her thoughts circled back to the fact that Edmund was gone, and that life, somehow, had to go on.

When the service was done, the coffin was carried out to be interred in the family crypt, and all of the mourners filed out of the church after it, to stand, blinking, in the winter sun.

The light reflected blindingly off the snow, but there was no warmth in it. Lady Chester slipped an arm around her daughter's waist, and led her gently to one side. Maria went, uncertain of what to do next. The Dowager stood for a moment, watching the coffin carried away, then a wail escaped her, the sound of the grief that she had held sternly in check in the days since Edmund's death, days in which she had locked herself away from the world.

Then, in a sudden flurry of movement, she spun, and rushed to stand before Maria. Through the black gauzy cloth of her veil, Maria saw her face contorted, her eyes glittering with irrational rage.

"You! This is your fault, you faithless strumpet. You poisoned him, I know it, poisoned him with those 'herbal remedies' of yours. You probably caused his fall in the first place somehow! I wouldn't put it past you. No doubt so that you could run off with your common lover! Lewis, isn't it? I wouldn't be surprised if you've been consorting with those terrible highwaymen too, putting all of our lives at risk! To think that my son, an Earl, should die, so that you might cavort with the gatekeeper's son! May you burn in the fires of hell for your actions!"

Silence surrounded them. Everyone stared, shocked by the Dowager's grief-stricken outburst. And in many eyes, doubt began to grow. Maria could see it – the moment when they all began to wonder if the Dowager's words held truth. She glanced around, a sense of panic growing in her – this could not be happening! She could not be so accused, at her husband's funeral, and in front of the entire district! Then, as the whispers began, the woman who had sat beside the Dowager stepped forward, wailing herself.

"I knew it, knew it! from the first moment I set eyes on her. She's a witch, a witch, mixing evil potions. A witch." The woman's voice rose to a shrill pitch, and the hovering townspeople moved closer, soaking in the drama of the moment. The old woman was still ranting, wailing, and her voice rose again over the whispers that now surrounded them. "A witch, I tell you, and the good Lord said 'Thou shalt not suffer a witch to live' – we should not tolerate her presence, for she has brought Lord Granville his death!"

The villagers gasped, and Maria swayed on her feet, the world going grey around her. Then a hand touched her shoulder, and a man stepped past her. Charles' voice was hard as he spoke, in a cold, measured tone.

"Ladies, these are very serious allegations that you have laid upon Lady Granville. Surely, if you are willing to state such a grievous charge, you are also able to bring forth reasonable evidence to support it? If you cannot, then all sensible people must reach the conclusion that this is malicious and vexatious behaviour, with no basis in reality." Hearing Charles' warm voice speak so passionately in her defence brought tears of gratitude to Maria's eyes. She drew herself up, leaning into her mother's steadying arm, and waited to see what would happen next.

After a moment of utter silence, everyone around them spoke at once. The Dowager and the old woman shouting further accusations, the townspeople debating amongst themselves, some supporting Maria, others not, the servants from Myniard House whispering amongst themselves nervously. For what was supposed to be a quiet, respectful, and sacred ceremony of farewell to a soul departing the earth, this had become a verbal brawl worthy of the lowest tavern.

After a few moments, another voice rose above them all.

"Silence!!! This is disgraceful behaviour from everyone."

"Who're you, to tell us what to do?"

The coarse voice came from the back of the crowd. Maria watched as Hunter drew himself up to his most impressive, and turned to glare at the speaker.

"I am the Duke of Melton. I might have expected such behaviour from the ignorant, or from drunkards in a tavern, but I do not expect such behaviour from Ladies of rank, nor from the good, respectable people of this town. I command you all to silence. The Earl of Granville is even now being laid in the family crypt – he deserves your respect. Go home, and do not speculate on these false accusations against his widow any further. Allow that the Dowager Countess is overwrought with her grief, and needs your kindness. Now go."

The townspeople fell silent, then a few whispers drifted amongst them, before they each bowed or curtseyed towards the Dowager and left. Once the churchyard was empty of all but Maria and her family, and the Dowager and her companion, the silence stretched. The Dowager stared at Maria, ignoring those around her, then spoke, her voice full of hatred.

"You've not heard the last of this. I will make sure that your vile acts are revealed, if it's the last thing I do. Come, Mrs Morton, please accompany me – I need at least one friendly face in my home at this difficult time."

She took the old woman's arm, and they turned their backs on everyone, and went to the Dowager's carriage. In silence, Maria stood, and watched until the carriage was out of sight.

~~~~~

Back at Myniard House, Maria was glad to discover that the Dowager had retired to her rooms, accompanied by Mrs Morton – a woman who had, it seemed, been Edmund's nurse when he was a small child, and had retained some influence with the family since. Thompson showed them all into the parlour, looking enquiringly at Maria.

"Please have some tea and biscuits sent up, Thompson, and I believe that the gentlemen may feel the need of a brandy at this point."

"Yes, my Lady."

They settled onto chairs, and nothing was said until the refreshments had been delivered, and the staff had left the room. Maria looked at those around her, and found strength in the warmth in Charles' eyes. He had, so long ago it seemed now, offered to help her. Well, she needed help now. She found the courage to speak.

"What can I do? I only ever tried to help Edmund live! And as to the other accusations... well, I have met Lewis twice, just twice, when I walked down the lane near the gatekeeper's cottage to pick herbs. He introduced himself, and was polite, if a little overfriendly, but I simply spoke the least I could, and left his presence immediately. But... if the townsfolk believe this of me, what might they do?"

"We will defend you, do not fear – and how can they pursue these accusations, when there is no evidence whatsoever that you ever did anything wrong?"

Hunter spoke with assurance, but Maria was not so easily convinced.

"I am afraid... but I refuse to be bested by the Dowager. She has made my life a misery for too long."

"But Maria darling, surely you don't mean to stay here, now that your husband is buried? Surely you will come home to live with us, at least until your mourning year is over?" Lady Chester clasped her daughter's hand, where she sat beside her on the couch, her face a picture of concern. Maria scanned the faces of those gathered around her, then met her mother's eyes.

"But I must stay here, no matter how much I might wish to be elsewhere. For if I leave, those who half believe the Dowager's words will be convinced of my guilt – they will say that I have run from here to avoid the truth being revealed! And I will not suffer my reputation to be besmirched by two old women's malicious accusations. I will go only when I feel able to do so without the appearance of having run away. After all, if people think on it, it will become obvious that I could not have planned to kill Edmund, for it was an accident, the fall from his horse, which led to him near drowning in the river, then catching the lung infection that was the death of him in the end!" For a moment, everyone sat in silence, considering her words. Then Charles moved to crouch before her, taking the hand that her mother was not holding in his, for a moment.

"My Lady, I believe that you are right, that you should stay, and defy their expectations. But, will you tell us what you know of the accident? I would have us prepared to answer any wild accusations they may bring, if you are to weather this storm well."

The warmth in his eyes made Maria feel warm all over, and she tightened her fingers on his. His eyes widened, and his fingers gently returned the pressure. If only, she thought, Edmund had ever looked at her like that.

"I... I was not present, obviously, so I can only tell you what the groom told me. The fox and hounds had managed to cross the river at a point not suitable for the horses. They rode fast to the bridge, and the horses were slipping on the icy stones, then, on the bridge, for no reason that the groom could see, Edmund's horse bucked and reared, slipping on the ice as it did so, and Edmund fell. He hit his head hard on the stone coping of the bridge, then tumbled over and fell into the icy waters of the river below. By the time they pulled him out, he was half drowned, and shaking as if with an ague. They carried him home on a makeshift hurdle."

"Can you tell us anything else? What did the physician say, when he saw Edmund? I am assuming that the physician was called immediately?"

"Yes, he was called. He cleaned the cut on Edmund's head, and said that he could not tell if there was internal damage, if his mind might not be affected. And he told us to keep him warm, and pray that he did not take an infection to the lungs, lest it become consumption. But it seems that was exactly what happened, despite our efforts." Charles nodded, and, as he thought, Hunter spoke quietly.

"It seems strange to me that Edmund's horse behaved as the groom described – for surely he would not have been riding a horse prone to wild fits of bucking and rearing? And slippery ground is not enough for a normally well-behaved horse to suddenly become wild – no other rider's horse did so, did they?"

"No, the other horses were all fairly steady, from what the groom said. And that was Edmund's favourite horse. It was, to the best of my knowledge, normally well behaved, and Edmund was a skilled rider."

Charles spoke again, sounding puzzled.

"Then... why did the horse behave as it did? What happened to it, after it bolted, once Edmund had fallen? Was there any evidence of a cause for the behaviour?"

Utter silence greeted this question, and Maria met Charles' eyes with a startled expression.

Chapter Ten

"A very good question indeed." Hunter came to stand near Charles, and spoke with a half amused, half pondering tone. "As a family, we never have been able to leave a puzzle alone, have we?"

"No. And this seems to me a very great puzzle – and one which may have a significant influence on Lady Granville's life."

Maria's voice came, softly, uncertain, and Charles returned his attention to her, tightening his fingers around hers again, his heart aching at the signs of stress and exhaustion in her face.

"I... I did not think to ask at the time, and no-one has ever said anything. Should we summon the groom, and ask him?"

"Yes, I believe that would be appropriate."

Charles stood, stepping to the side to pull the bell rope, and summon a footman. Soon, there was a tap on the door, and a footman entered.

"Yes, my Lady?"

Maria gave a wry smile, as if the staff turning to her was an unusual occurrence. Charles wondered, again, what her life had been like in this house.

"Please bring the groom, who was in attendance on my late husband on the day of the hunt, to speak to me now."

The footman looked rather startled at this request, but bowed.

"As you wish, my Lady. I will return with him as soon as I locate him."

Charles paced about the room – the more he thought about the situation, the more convinced he became that there was far more to this matter of Lord Granville's horse suddenly behaving so uncharacteristically than had been assumed. Perhaps he was overthinking it, and it was simply the Dowager Countess' shocking accusation of foul play that was leading his thoughts astray, but he struggled to convince himself of that. But what might cause a normally reasonable horse to behave so?

They turned their attention to the refreshments, no-one really wanting to eat, yet knowing that they should. The silence stretched as they waited. Maria's father, Lord Chester, stood, and joined Charles in pacing about the room, muttering to himself.

"Right rum business this! How dare that woman accuse my daughter of murder! We'll see this cleared up, can't have the family name besmirched, or the innocent accused!"

Charles could only agree with his sentiments. Maria sat, quiet, her eyes sad, her posture showing clearly how much of a toll all of this was taking on her.

Charles wanted, more than anything else, to simply take her in his arms, to hold her, to make her safe, to take the sadness and fear away. It was not his place to do so. As he watched her, he knew that he would do everything he could, no matter what it took, to one day make it his place to care for her. But this was not the time to think or speak of such things, so soon after her husband's death, and with the shadow of accusation hanging over her.

After a blessedly short time, the footman returned, a nervous looking groom following him.

"Here he is, my Lady. This is Dickins. He was with them, the day of..."

"Thank you."

The footman bowed and left, looking curious, and as if he would desperately like to stay, to discover what was about to be said.

"Dickins – please, take a seat. We'd like to ask you a few questions about Lord Granville's accident."

At Charles' words, Dickins looked uncertainly at Maria, who simply nodded, and waved him to a chair. He sat, perched on the edge, twisting his cap between his fingers.

"First, please tell us what happened that day, as best you remember."

Dickins thought a moment, then spoke, repeating almost exactly what Maria had told them of the events of the day. Charles waited until he had finished telling of the moments after they had brought Lord Granville back to the house.

"Dickins, what of the horse? You have said that Lord Granville's horse ran off, bolting away down the road, immediately after Lord Granville fell. But what happened to it after that?"

Dickins twisted his cap into a tight wad of cloth, looking down, as if afraid.

"My Lord... I... at the time, I was more concerned about getting Lord Granville out of the river, and home. I didn't chase off after his horse, even thought, mayhap, I should have." He hesitated, as if expecting to be chastised for his failure. When no criticism came, he took a deep breath and went on. "After, I went back to look, but I couldn't find him. The forest is thick near there, and he had run off that way. Two weeks ago, the woodcutter brought me his saddle – he'd found it, lying in a clearing deep in the woods. The girth was snapped, and the saddle all scratched up, like. But that's the only sign of the horse we've had."

"Why didn't you tell us?"

Maria looked at the man, puzzled. He twisted the cap even tighter, and looked away, fidgeting on the edge of his chair, before meeting her eyes.

"My Lady, if I'm t' be honest with you, because I was afraid. Afraid that her Ladyship would turn me off, for losing an expensive horse, or even, perhaps, blame me for what the horse did, given I was caring for it. So, I kept hoping he'd turn up, and I'd never have t' tell her."

Maria's eyes lit with what Charles could only describe as heartfelt sympathy. She sighed, and nodded sadly, as if the man's words were not at all unexpected.

"I understand, Dickins. I do not blame you. Do you think... do you think that, with help, you could find the horse?"

"Perhaps, my Lady, it's been many weeks now, but it's possible. But... won't her Ladyship..."

"We will deal with that, should the situation occur. I guarantee that you will not be turned off and left with nowhere to go."

Charles' voice was hard. He was, truth to tell, a little shocked – that the Dowager Countess invoked such fear in her staff, that this man believed she would blame him, for things which he manifestly could not have affected – this horrified him, and made him wonder just how she had treated Maria. Fragments of their conversation at the wedding breakfast came back to him, and made far more sense now, than they had then.

"Thank you, my Lord."

"We'll start the search tomorrow, then. We'll come to you in the stables, in the morning. Now, you'd best be back to your duties."

Dickins rose, bowed, and almost ran from the room.

~~~~

The following day, Hunter, Charles and Kevin, Maria's brother, decided to split up – Hunter and Kevin to seek out some of the men who had been participants in the ill-fated hunt, and Charles to go with Dickins and other grooms to search for the horse. As Charles and the grooms set off from the stables, a man came hurrying up the drive.

Charles stopped, and waited as he approached.

"Who might you be?"

"Lewis Maddox, my Lord."

"Lewis? The gatekeeper's son?"

Charles' voice had risen, his memory of the previous day's accusations returning in detail.

'Yes, my Lord. I am told that I have been falsely accused of the worst kind of behaviour. I greatly respect Lady Granville, I would never... I came here to apologise for my very existence, that it should have been used to harm her in such a way. I do not know what I can do to help lay these terrible accusations against her to rest, but I wish to help in any way that I can."

Charles relaxed a little – the man seemed genuine, and as horrified as they were at the words that had been spoken yesterday.

"As it happens, you can help. It seems that Lord Granville's horse was never recovered, after it bolted from the scene of his accident. We are off to search the forests for it. Your assistance will be welcome. Come with us."

Lewis joined them, and they set off. It was, in the end, a long, tedious, and fruitless day of searching. By the time they returned, dusk was closing in. The grooms hurried to carry out their normal duties, Lewis left them as they passed the gatekeeper's cottage, and Charles took himself into the house, the thought of food and drink a most welcome one.

Hunter and Kevin had also returned, and waited for him in the parlour, with everyone else.

"Did you have any success?"

Maria's eyes met his, full of hope. He hated to disappoint her.

"No, not yet, unfortunately. We did find a few scraps of leather, likely once part of the horse's bridle, but no sign of the horse. We won't give up, we will go out again tomorrow. One interesting thing did happen however. As we set off, we were joined by an unexpected helper. Lewis Maddox."

Maria gasped.

"Why...?"

"He had come to apologise – he had heard of what was said at the funeral, and deeply regrets that his name has been used to besmirch your name. He offered to help."

"I am glad. Whilst he made me uncomfortable, I never thought that he meant me any ill. But perhaps he should talk to his stepmother about the evils of gossip."

"Maddox? I remember that name. I believe he did well for himself in France, a worthy and honourable soldier. I am sure that I met him, during the war."

Hunter looked thoughtful, staring into the distance as he cast his mind back.

"That is good to know. He certainly put in the effort today. But enough of my day – what success did you have?"

"More than you! We managed to speak to four of the men who were present at the accident. All of them agree that the horse acted most unusually. They knew the animal, and it had never done anything like that before."

Maria spoke into the silence that followed Hunter's words.

"Then... we are right to suspect that there is more to it than everyone assumed? I do not know if that pleases me, or frightens me."

"Yes, it seems clear that it was, perhaps, no accident at all. We will keep investigating, until we have an answer. But tell me – has the Dowager spoken to you today?"

Charles was concerned that Maria might have been forced to endure more accusations, and was relieved when she shook her head, and Lady Chester replied to his question.

"No. Thankfully that unpleasant woman has not stirred from her rooms. Sensible of her, in my opinion. She may live in this house, but she is certainly not welcome in our company."

"Good, I must agree with you. It will be best for everyone if she stays secluded for some time. Now, I must admit to being rather hungry, after a day traipsing through the woods..."

As he spoke, Thompson tapped on the door, and announced that dinner was ready. Everyone laughed, the apposite timing breaking the rather sombre mood of the conversation. In the dining room, Charles found himself seated next to Maria, and glanced at her sidelong – she caught his eye and smiled at him, a little uncertain. Even so small a smile made him feel warm all over. As the servants busied themselves serving the first course, he could not resist, he reached out and took her hand, where it lay on her lap, beneath the table. Her eyes widened, but she said nothing, simply returning the pressure of his fingers. For now, it was enough. But he knew that he wanted more – for years to come.

∼∼∼∼∼

Each day of the following week was much the same. Eventually, Hunter and Kevin had spoken to every man who had been present at the time of Lord Granville's fall – they all agreed that what had happened was most out of the expected way. Charles and his party of searchers had covered a vast area of the local countryside, and were almost at the point of despair.

"One last day of searching, and then we may have to give up. I would not have thought that a single horse would have wandered so far. Perhaps he was found by the gypsies, and is long gone from hereabouts – I don't know, but I have to try one more time."

"Perhaps, if we come with you today, we can cover even more ground."

Charles looked at Hunter gratefully, and nodded.

When they had left, Maria picked up the embroidery she had been working on, and forced herself to continue. If she had to just sit here and wait for many more days, she would go completely mad. She had ventured out to her cottage once, to make certain that her herbs and simples were still as they should be, but the winter cold had made her glad to return to the house. If only there were more to do, than read, embroider, and talk to her mother and Nerissa! Her father, of course, had shut himself away in the library.

But the day eventually drew towards dusk, and the welcome sound of the men returning. They came through the door, and she rose, hope on her face at the sight of their smiles.

"Have you...?"

"Yes, yes! We found the beast. Halfway to the next county, but alive, standing there picking at the grass through the snow, in a sheltered forest clearing. And we were right to worry about the cause of him rearing and bucking that day. For across his upper flank, there is a wound – unhealed, deep, and oozing. It is the sort of wound that could only have been made by a barbed dart or perhaps an arrow."

Charles voice was full of the pleasure of having his belief proven true, but Maria was not so sure, she went to him, and, without thought, took his hands.

"How can you be sure? Could not a branch in the forest...?"

Hunter smiled at them both, and shook his head.

"No – I have seen entirely too many wounds from arrows and every other weapon you might imagine, whilst in France and Spain. This looks as if a barbed dart was the cause, and it was stuck in the flesh for some time, before tearing free. I think that we can safely say that someone wanted Lord Granville dead, or at the least, injured." Maria felt her stomach churn, and her hands tightened on Charles'. Fear rushed through her – who? Why? And would the Dowager, or that horrible Morton woman, try to blame her for this too? Hunter's next words echoed her concern. "The question, of course, is who? We know that Maria did not want her husband dead, no matter what the Dowager has said – but who did? And why?"

Chapter Eleven

The next day, as he walked into the town, Charles was still asking himself that question. He had found himself needing to get out, away from the stifling atmosphere of tension in Myniard House, to move, to think, and had decided to see what was being said in the town. It seemed that most of the district felt the need to go shopping, for the main street was crowded, and small clusters of people stopped to talk along the way.

Every group that Charles passed, he heard snippets of conversation – most still about the events at the funeral, and full of supposition and exaggeration. He sighed heavily as he passed yet another gossiping group and turned into the open door of the shop that sold ribbons, bonnets, and the like – he had hoped for something better, but had not really expected anything different. He would ignore them all, and buy Maria a small gift for her birthday tomorrow, then return to Myniard House.

"Sigh worthy indeed! They are all petty-minded gossips with nothing better to do!"

Charles turned to the woman who had spoken, curious. She was older, arrayed in a hat and gown that would have been the height of fashion twenty years before. She waved her hand expressively at the group he had just passed.

"My Lady, impolite as it is of me to do so, I must agree with you. Charles Barrington, Viscount Wareham, at your service."

He bowed. She looked at him with an arch expression, then favoured him with a broad smile.

"I am Lady Fremont. My property adjoins Myniard Park. Do I have it correct that you are some relative of Lady Granville's?"

"Not exactly - my brother married her sister. She was my neighbour in childhood. I have come with my brother and his wife to support her at this difficult time."

"Very laudable of you. I don't believe a word of the accusations. Lucy Morton has always been one to stir up trouble – in her opinion, no woman would ever really have been good enough for Lord Granville. And as for Constance... that's the elder Lady Granville – well, she kept her son right under her thumb – and when he chose his own wife... you can imagine the result."

"Thank you for not believing the accusations. I wish more people were as clear sighted as you."

She smiled at Charles again, as if being called clearsighted amused her.

"Most round here wouldn't call me that. But thank you for doing so. They think I'm a little addle witted, because I spend my time studying the stars. Ignorant. That's what they are."

"The stars?"

"Yes, I've a telescope on top of the old tower on my land. I spend most evenings up there – despite the ghosts."

"Ghosts?"

Charles was beginning to wonder where this conversation was going, but he could not exactly simply walk away. Best to let the woman ramble on if she wanted to.

"Ghosts. In the cellar of my tower, and, I believe, in that old Dower House on Myniard Park. I keep seeing dark shapes going in and out of there at night, and strange lights in the windows. The place has been abandoned and crumbling for twenty years or more, since the previous Lord Granville's mother died. So, it has to be ghosts, doesn't it?"

"Errr, I suppose so. If it's been abandoned for twenty years."

"I knew you were an intelligent young man – knew it the second I heard you sigh at the gossips. Well, I must be off about my day. Do enjoy your visit here, as much as you can in the circumstances."

She waved her hand at him, and set off down the street. Charles watched her go, bemused, then turned back into the shop – what could he buy for Maria, that would still be appropriate for her to wear during mourning? Not that it was really appropriate for him to be buying her anything, but propriety be damned – he wanted to cheer her up, if he could.

~~~~

Maria sat, staring at the parcel in her hand.

A parcel addressed to her, and delivered by a man in the livery of one of the most famous jewellers in London. She was almost afraid to open it. She sat in the conservatory of Myniard House, escaping the winter chill for a short while, surrounded by the small number of flowers that the gardeners could convince to bloom, even in winter, in the warmth of the glass enclosed room. Still she shivered. Then she shook herself out of her irrational fear, and began to open the parcel.

The jewellers box was carved, ornate. But no more ornate than the beautiful necklace revealed when she opened it. She gasped, reaching a careful finger to trace its gems and pearls, all set into an elegant pattern in gold. As she did, her hand brushed the inside of the lid of the box, and a folded and sealed note fell out. She lifted it, and turned it to study the seal.

Her face paled, and her breath stopped for a moment. It bore Edmund's seal. How was this possible?

Shaking, she broke the seal.

My darling Maria,

I pray that this gift pleases you, on your birthday. I beg your forgiveness – for so many things. Especially for my weakness, my failure to defend you from my mother. It shames me that I have let things be as they are, for so long.

But I have begun something that will free us. I have begun work to restore the Dower House, that my mother might move there, and rule her own household, leaving you to rule yours — for it is, and should always have been yours, from the moment I married you.

Forgive me?

Edmund.

Her tears blinded her. He must have arranged this while they were in London, months before. He had, after all, actually loved her. To find out now, so much too late... She sat, and let the tears fall, crying for everything that had happened, from the moment she had met Edmund, for the loss of all her childish illusions, the heartbreak of the way her marriage had been, and the heartbreak of knowing, now, that despite all his faults, her husband had loved her. Loved her, when she had never, truly loved him. Guilt crushed her, and she sobbed harder.

She had come here to be alone, leaving the others to continue their discussion about who might have set out to injure Edmund, and the footman had met her in the hall, parcel in hand. She was so glad that he had not found her in the parlour, for she needed this time to cry, to grieve. How could she forgive herself?

A small sound caught her attention, and she lifted her tear streaked face. Concerned hazel eyes met hers, and she flushed, unsure what to do, or say. He came towards her, dropping onto the seat beside her.

"My Lady... Maria... what is the matter? What has happened to bring you to tears?"

At his words, the tears flowed harder again, and she turned her face away, one hand clutching the box in her lap until her knuckles were white. Gentle arms enfolded her, pulling her to rest against the hard warmth of his chest. It was too much – she had longed for such a touch, for so long, had cried herself to sleep so often, that now, when she was already distraught, to be held so gently overwhelmed her. She cried, her tears soaking the front of his jacket, cried for everything she had lost, every dream that had been shattered, every cruel word from the Dowager that she had not known how to deal with. And he held her through it all, until, finally, the tears slowed and stopped. For a moment longer, she stayed there, safe in the curve of his arms, before she drew herself up. He released her, allowing her the choice, and waited.

"I..." she released the box, leaving it lie in her lap, and smoothed the note which was crumpled in her hand. She held it out to him, turning the box so that he might see what it contained. "This. It came inside this box, with this gift."

He took the note from her, the passing touch of his fingers on hers sending heat shooting through her, and lifted it to read. She watched his face as he read, watched him then turn his eyes to the beautiful necklace in the box, and met those eyes when they finally returned to her face.

"It is beautiful, as you are. I can see, from his choice, that he understood what would suit you. It is a pity that he never found the courage, in life, to defy his mother, to allow you to have the marriage you deserved. But at least now you know that he tried, that he had begun work to improve things."

"Yes, but... I..." she could not say it, not even to Charles.

"You never loved him, did you? You accepted his offer, because your parents said it was an excellent match."

How did he know? It startled her, that he should, so easily, go to the heart of her sorrow.

"I did not love him. You are right. And, now that I know that he did love me, to the best of his ability, I feel so guilty, so sad. I wish I had known, while he still lived. I had no idea that he had commissioned work on the Dower House! But now, it is all too late, and worst of all, whilst I grieve for him, for the fact that someone's terrible actions meant that he died well before his time, I cannot, truly, say that I am sorry that he is gone – for it frees me, in a way. I have the choice, once these accusations are dealt with, to walk away from this place, from the Dowager Countess. I will not need to deal with whatever cousin inherits the title, for I have the choice to return to my parent's home. Am I a reprehensible person, to feel so?"

She waited, afraid that he would condemn her for her inappropriate feelings, afraid that this man, whose opinion mattered more to her than anyone's, she realised, would turn from her. Yet she could not bring herself to lie to him, to pretend to feelings which she did not have. As she watched, he carefully folded the note, and placed it in the box, closing the lid on the beautiful glitter of the necklace.

His hands sought hers, and he brought her cold fingers to his lips, kissing them gently, his eyes never leaving hers. When he finally spoke, his voice was rough with emotion.

"I would never call you reprehensible. Instead, I think you brave, and I respect you for having the courage to admit to your true feelings, no matter that they are not what society believes they should be. You have, from what I have seen this last week, suffered terribly, not just now, but throughout your marriage. The Dowager is not, from all indications, a pleasant person to live with. I have always thought you beautiful, in soul, not just in body, and nothing will ever change that."

His obvious sincerity brought tears to her eyes again. He reached out, cupping her cheek in his palm, his thumb gently brushing the tears aside, and leant forward until his lips met hers. It was the softest, briefest of kisses, yet the warmth that spread from that contact burned through her as if she stood in a bonfire. This, this sensation, was the sort of thing she had dreamed of, when, as a naïve girl, she had imagined love and marriage. That she should feel it now, with this man who she had known all her life, now, when propriety mandated that she spend the next year in mourning, living quietly away from society, was the greatest irony.

She said nothing, but her eyes clung to his, her heart beating faster. He sat back, his hands now resting in his lap. They were the picture of propriety now. Maria wanted to laugh, in an odd, self-deprecating way, so impossible did her situation seem. Charles, having allowed himself to look away, was still, staring into the distance. She had seen him like this before – he was thinking, worrying at some problem – her? Or something else? She did not know. She simply waited.

After some minutes he spoke.

"Maria... in this note Edmund mentions beginning to repair the Dower House – which means that he had begun that long before his accident, before you came to London for Hunter's wedding, doesn't it?"

"Yes, that must be so, for him to mention it here."

He nodded, as if she had just confirmed some significant thing, then after lifting her hand to his lips, and pressing a gentle kiss to her palm, he rose, bowed, and turned to go.

"I will return as soon as I can."

~~~~

Charles strode from the conservatory, his mind in turmoil. She had allowed him a kiss! However fleeting, however inappropriate, she had allowed it. He wanted far more than that one soft kiss. The feel of her in his arms as she had cried bitter tears had left him wanting to hold her forever, to soothe away her distress, to keep her safe. He could not, not yet, for, no matter what they both might come to wish, what he most desperately hoped they would come to wish, he could do nothing obvious until her year of mourning was over.

But, the seemingly minor detail of the repair of the Dower House, contained in Edmund's note which had come with the necklace, had begun a very different chain of thought in his mind, when combined with the Dowager's ravings at the funeral, which were branded in his memory, and the eccentric ramblings of Lady Fremont, just that morning.

For Lady Fremont had mentioned the Dower House on Myniard Park, and strange comings and goings. Charles had disregarded her spiritualist assertion that there were ghosts – and now, just perhaps, another explanation presented itself. An explanation which, if true, would be the key to proving that Maria had not intended her husband any harm.

Fifteen minutes later, Charles, Hunter and Kevin were ahorse, and on their way to the old Dower House.

Chapter Twelve

Maria sat for some time after Charles had gone, her fingers gently touching her lips, her mind reeling with the possibilities which flowed from that kiss. Perhaps her life was not so bleak as she had thought. Perhaps, once her year of mourning was done, there was a chance for happiness. She should not put so much freight of hope upon one kiss, yet she could not stop herself. In the end, she wiped the last traces of tears from her face, and gathering up the box, went to her rooms. It was time that she joined the others again, and got on with life.

Half an hour later, feeling far more hopeful about life in general, she entered the parlour, to find her parents and Nerissa talking.

"I don't know, these young men, haring off after some idea, with barely a moment's notice. All too energetic for me!"

Lord Chester sipped a brandy, and shook his head. Maria had to assume that he spoke of Charles, Hunter, and Kevin, for they were absent from the room.

"Where have they gone, Father?"

"I've no idea – they didn't even wait to explain. Rash, too rash, still, age will calm them down eventually."

Maria simply nodded, and dropped onto the couch beside Nerissa – there really wasn't much she could say in response. She pulled her embroidery from the basket she had left there earlier, and tried to focus her attention on the quality of her stitches. That proved far more difficult than usual, as the question of where the men had gone nagged at her. When she had almost given up on her needlework, the door opened, without even a knock, and a sharp voice destroyed the last of her concentration.

"How disappointing. I had hoped that all of the unwelcome guests would have departed by now. It seems I must still share my home with the faithless strumpet and her relatives. Mark my words, you will pay for your deeds – do not think, for a moment, that I will ever relent."

The Dowager stood in the room, glaring at everyone. Maria found herself shaking – with both fear and anger. Lord Chester carefully placed his brandy glass on the side table and stood, drawing himself up to his most imposing.

"Whatever you may believe, my Lady, nothing justifies your rudeness, nor your wholly inappropriate treatment of my daughter. I will thank you to remember that, and keep a civil tongue in your head. I respect your grief, but it is not an excuse for these baseless and vicious accusations."

"Are you accusing me of lying? How dare you! I will not stay to be spoken to like this."

She turned, and stormed out of the room. There was stunned silence. After a moment, Nerissa stifled a laugh.

"Oh dear, what an unpleasant woman she is! But… I have formed the impression that no one has ever defied her, or challenged her words and manner, and she does not cope with it well at all. Is that the way of it Maria?"

"Yes, dear sister, I believe you have the right of it. Sadly, my husband never really stood up to her, and I, I am ashamed to admit, did not have the strength to argue, day after day."

Nerissa nodded.

"Then I am quite certain that she will not enjoy the next few weeks, for I cannot imagine that we can, or will, permit her to continue in this manner. And once we have proved your innocence, you can leave here, and never see that terrible woman again."

"I hope that you are right, that we can prove her wrong, soon, for I fully admit that I will not regret leaving this place, never to return."

"I believe that we are all in agreeance with that sentiment."

Lady Chester's voice was soft, but carried, very clearly, her loathing for the situation.

~~~~~

The grooms had provided directions to the old Dower House, and they soon saw it, amongst the trees in the distance, once they came out of the trail through the woods.

The day was clear, but clouds were rolling in as the afternoon progressed – there would likely be more snow that night. Their horses' hooves crunching on the snow were the only sounds in the clearing that surrounded the dilapidated building. Charles slipped to the ground, and walked forward, closely examining the area, and the walls of the place.

The recent repairs to some of the stonework were obvious, but the work was equally obviously incomplete, no doubt stopped for the duration of winter. On the other side of the building there was what had once been a gravelled drive, which led past one side to a very much unrepaired stable. They left their horses tethered in the meagre shelter, and turned back to the Dower House itself.

"Exactly what are we looking for, Charles?"

Kevin had been very willing to be pulled out of the house, and into action, but curiosity was eating at him.

"I'm not sure. But, if I'm correct, we'll find signs of men, other than the stonemasons, having been here, perhaps of people having camped here, or even goods stored here."

"And why would we find that?"

"Well, I may be drawing a very long bow here, but it's the only even vaguely likely idea I've come up with. We wanted a reason for someone to want Lord Granville injured or dead. And there was simply nothing. But what I have discovered today, when taken in conjunction with the Dowager's ravings at the funeral, has provided a possible explanation. Highwaymen."

"Highwaymen? What on earth has that to do with any of it? And with this house?"

"Let me give you the facts, as I know them. Old Lady Fremont, who I met quite by accident in the town this morning, is a close neighbour. She's obsessed with studying the stars, and her neighbours, through her telescope, which is installed on top of that old tower over there, on her property." Charles pointed at the top of an old stone tower, where it rose above the treetops. "She claims that tower, and this house, are haunted. That she sees dark figures going in and out of here at evening, and strange lights. I thought her simply eccentric, until I remembered the Dowager's mention of highwaymen. Then I wondered if there were actual highwaymen, who needed a place to hide away, and to hide the items they stole."

"Hmmm, that seems feasible – but what has that to do with Lord Granville's death, and proving Maria innocent?"

"This morning a parcel was delivered to Myniard House, for Maria. It was a birthday gift, that her husband had arranged, months ago when they were in London, and it came with a note in his hand. A note in which, amongst other things, he told her that he was having the Dower House repaired, that he might cause his mother to move here, and allow Maria to finally rule her own home."

"Again, what has that to do with Lord Granville's death?"

"Well... if this has been used by highwaymen as a secret place to hide – themselves and their ill-gotten gains – then they would not be best pleased by him wanting to get it repaired and get his mother living here, would they? How far would they go, to save themselves from discovery, and the hangman's noose, once they knew what he planned?"

"Well reasoned!"

Hunter looked approvingly at his brother, as Kevin thought it all through.

"So, you think that the highwaymen discovered what my sister's husband was doing, and, in desperation to save themselves from discovery, they took action to stop him, in the most absolute way?"

"That is exactly what I think. But if we find no evidence of them here, or in the cellars of old Lady Fremont's tower, then all of my reasoning will be for naught – we won't be able to prove anything. So I want to search the place."

Both Kevin and Hunter nodded.

"Let's be about it then."

Kevin went to move towards the house.

"Wait."

Hunter looked around him, studying the once gravelled drive where they stood.

"For a place that has been long abandoned, and only seen a small number of stonemason's men recently, this drive is a churn of uneven surfaces – it shows mud and ruts more like a carter's yard, as if many carts have been in and out of here recently – so perhaps you are right. Let's hope that what is inside confirms it."

They went inside, studying everything around them, and set about searching every part of the house. It was obvious how beautiful a residence it had once been, and how sad a condition it had fallen to. It was also obvious that others had been there recently – muddy footprints on marble, food scraps in the kitchen and more.

But nothing to conclusively prove it any more than the stonemasons at work. Until they reached the cellars. The first was empty, but at its rear, they discovered a partly obscured door which led into further rooms. Rooms which were full of an odd assortment of items, all of significant worth, jumbled together in boxes and bags. No legitimate house would store priceless jewellery and weaponry in a jumble in the cellar – this had to be contraband.

"Don't disturb it. Leave it as close to exactly as we found it as possible. We mustn't let them realise that we've been here."

"Good thinking, Charles. I assume that you want us to set a watch on the place, and be ready to apprehend them, when they return?"

"Yes."

"Let's hope that's not too far in the future, then. I have a growing abhorrence for this place." Hunter looked at the clutter of valuables before them with distaste. "Let's be away back to Myniard House then, and get that arranged, making sure that we've covered our tracks here well. That snow laden cloud will serve us well, by covering the horses' tracks if we're lucky."

They moved, scuffing the dust of the cellar floors to remove their footprints, and slipped out of the house, leaving it as it had been when they arrived. The horses were glad to be moving again, and they spent the ride back to Myniard House, through the beginning of the snowfall, planning a schedule for keeping watch on the Dower House.

At Myniard House, they sent a groom back to watch the Dower House immediately, and went in to inform the others of their plan.

~~~~~

The next week was frustrating for all. The Dowager moved through the house as if no one else existed, cutting them absolutely, sitting at the dinner table as if alone and resisting any attempt of anyone to speak to her. The staff moved around them all as if terrified – for the Dowager snapped at them, yet when she was not present, they were happy to serve Maria – unless the Dowager's commands and Maria's contradicted each other.

The watch on the Dower House continued, with no sign of any highwaymen yet, and Charles wondered if he was wrong, if there was some other explanation – yet his instinct said that he was right. Each day, when the grooms watching the place returned from their shift of observation, they came to the house to report. Finally, after a week of hearing about the Dower House, about the place that her husband had hoped would allow everything to change, Maria apparently reached a decision.

"I want to see this place, this house that, if you are correct, caused Edmund's death. Listening to you speak of it, every day, without knowing what it actually looks like, is impossible to bear, any longer. Please, take me there – let me see it with my own eyes."

Charles looked at Hunter and Kevin, unsure if this was a good idea. His first instinct was to say no, to protect Maria, to keep her as far from potential danger as possible. Kevin, gave him a wry grin, and shook his head gently.

"If she really wants to go, she'll worry at it until we give in. Maria was always the well behaved one, of all of us, but also the most stubborn, if she really wanted something. Best to give in."

Maria scowled at him, but could not really argue, as he was supporting her getting what she wanted. Charles nodded, sighing.

"This afternoon then – it's already late, but the day is clear – best to take advantage of the weather while we can. My Lady, if you would change into your riding habit?"

"Thank you."

She left the room, and Charles sent a footman to tell the grooms to prepare the horses, including Maria's.

~~~~

The cold crisp air stung her cheeks – no doubt they were red – and her breath came in misty puffs, but the day was still, the late afternoon sun dropping rapidly towards the horizon. Maria was glad to be outside, glad to shake off the oppressive air of the house, where the Dowager moved about them like a ghost, glaring at every step, or making snide comments, disguised as direction to the servants.

"We won't stay long – it will be dusk when we get there – just enough time for you to see the place before the light begins to fail completely."

Maria simply nodded, concentrating on the path through the woods.

Looking down at her skirt falling across her leg, and down over the horse's neck and side, she took joy in the fact that it wasn't black – it was a very dark green – just acceptable during mourning. She sighed, thinking of the tasks ahead – she had very few garments truly suited for mourning – she would need to order a whole new wardrobe for this year ahead. The thought of wearing nothing but black and dark greys for a year was instantly depressing.

They emerged from the trees into a small clearing, the late afternoon sun sparking glints off the ice rimed tree branches, and paused a moment at the sound of approaching hoofbeats. Seconds later, a groom rode into the clearing, moving at speed. He pulled the horse to a stop, narrowly avoiding a collision.

"My Lord, at the Dower House – two men just arrived, driving a cart – they're unloading things now. Hurry."

He turned and set off, back the way he had come. Charles cast a worried glance at Maria, as they surged into motion – but if they were to catch the men, there was no time to waste. Maria urged her horse forward, intent on keeping up.

They halted in the edge of the woods, within sight of the Dower House. A cart stood on the rutted drive, close to the house. They observed for a short while, as two men went back and forth, carrying boxes.

"We outnumber them – we should be able to take them – but where? What will give us the most advantage?"

Charles looked to Hunter as he spoke, wanting the advice that came from Hunter's experience at war. Hunter considered, watching the pattern of the men's movement.

"If we leave the horses here, so that any noise they make does not give us away, we should be able to trap them between us – two of us going in through the other side of the house, and two waiting behind the hedge here. And if Maria can hide behind that clump of bushes, where she can see both positions, she can signal when we are ready, so that we all move at the same time."

Charles looked at Maria again, concerned – and she knew that he would far rather leave her with the horses, as far from risk as possible – yet Hunter's plan made sense. Maria looked at Hunter, her eyes full of gratitude, glad that she was being treated as useful, rather than a hindrance.

"Very well then, let us get ourselves into position."

They tethered the horses in a clearing, a little back from the forest edge, and stealthily crept forward at a point when the men had just entered the house with their latest load of boxes. Once they were in place, Hunter signalled his readiness, and he and Kevin slipped in through the kitchen door of the house. Maria signalled to Charles and the groom, and they moved forward from the hedge towards the cart and the open front door.

All seemed calm, for a few seconds, then there was a loud crash from inside, and the two men came running out of the door. Charles and the groom were still some distance away. The men saw them, and turned, running frantically around the side of the house, and out across the overgrown lawn – straight towards Maria. She froze, suddenly panicked, uncertain of what to do, then rose, and turned, intending to run. She heard a thud, and looked back to see that the groom had succeeded in tackling one man to the ground.

Hunter and Kevin had just emerged from the front door and ran towards him. But the second man was still running, with Charles pursuing him – running now with even more purpose, straight for Maria. She turned, and fled, with the horrible sense that he would catch her – for she simply was not very fast, not as strong or fit as this man seemed.

Moments stretched to feel like hours, and her breath came ragged in her throat. She ran, wobbling over the uneven tussocks of long untended grass, dodging around bushes, but all with a sense of hopelessness – for she could hear the man getting closer, could hear his breath, and the thump of his feet on the ground.

A hand grabbed her arm, spinning her off balance, and her ankle twisted on the rough grass. She was jerked up, pulled against a hard body encased in coarsely woven cloth, and held.

"Well then, what have we here? I'd warrant that these fine gentlemen wouldn't want to see a pretty thing like you hurt, now would they?" Maria stayed silent, squirming a little in his grip, hoping that she might break free. He clasped her tighter, his fingers bruising her arm, and he laughed. "No, my little bird, you'll not get free of me so easily. Now – if you gentlemen would just release my partner there, and bring us two of your horses, then I'll consider releasing this lovely lady."

Charles had come to a halt, a short distance from them, anguish on his face. His eyes met hers, and Maria saw in them the truth of his feelings for her. Her heart sang – no matter how others might condemn him for it, no matter that so soon after her husband's death, such things were not to be considered, to know that she was loved was worth any danger.

Behind him, Hunter and Kevin had reached the groom, and were tying the captured man with rope taken from their cart. Charles held her eyes a little longer, giving a tiny shake of his head. She stilled completely, waiting. It seemed obvious to her that he had a plan, of some kind, to free her.

"I think not. I'm afraid that we won't be releasing either of you."

"Then the lady will suffer." His grip tightened on her arms again, as he twisted them behind her, and began to force her to move towards the woods. Maria gasped at the pain, and stumbled on the uneven ground, the increasing darkness making it hard to see where she trod. He hauled her up again, shaking her with annoyance. "Walk, woman, surely you can manage that?"

As he did so, he looked away from Charles to glare at Maria. Maria saw a flicker of movement, from the corner of her eye. She sagged in the man's grasp, as if her ankle had twisted completely, trying to look as helpless as possible.

"My ankle! I can't…"

He snarled at her, still attempting to make her stand, while her limp weight dragged at him. It was enough. Seconds later, Charles reached them. His fist slammed into the man's jaw, and, with a roar, the man dropped Maria and spun, flailing at Charles, unbalanced. A second punch from Charles dropped him to his knees, just as Hunter reached them, more rope in hand.

As Charles and Hunter bound the man tightly, Maria stood, carefully testing her ankle before taking a step. It hurt, but not impossibly. Her arms hurt more. She stepped forward, and looked down at the bound man, before turning away.

Charles came to her, reaching out to gently touch her shoulder.

"Maria... my Lady... I am so sorry, I should never have allowed... I should have been quicker..."

She turned to him, and took his hands.

"You should have done exactly as you did. You could not know that they would move out of the house that fast, nor that they would turn towards where I hid. I am more than grateful for the speed with which you saved me from that man."

He lifted her hand, and pressed his lips to it, just for a moment. Heat surged through her body, and her bruises seemed irrelevant in that moment.

"Thank you, my Lady. Will you be able to go to the old stable there, and find a place to sit, while we deal with these men?"

"Of course. Do what you must."

Charles turned, and went to the groom.

"Fetch the magistrate, as soon as you can. I'd have him see these men like this, with their stolen goods and cart exactly as it is."

"Yes, my Lord."

The groom went to regain his horse and set off down the lane into the darkness. Kevin had been into the house again, and found a lantern, which cast strange shadows about them as they brought the bound men to the cart, and settled to wait. Maria simply sat, watching, and shivered, as the fear and shock of the last hour caught up with her.

Chapter Thirteen

Charles, after ensuring that the men were secure, went to make certain that Maria was safe and well. At the sight of her shivering, he pulled off his coat, and dropped it around her shoulders. She looked at him gratefully. He wanted, in that instant, to pull her into his arms, to hold her against him, to keep her safe forever. He did not have the right to do so. So he sat beside her, content, for the time being, to simply talk, to discuss what should happen next.

"As soon as the magistrate arrives, and we can provide the initial information he needs, and hand these men over to him, I will escort you home. If the magistrate needs to speak to me further, he can do so tomorrow."

"I do not mind waiting. I want to see these men taken away. To know that Edmund's killers, for that is what they are, I believe, will be brought to justice."

"I understand – but I would not see you take a chill – the night is cold, and there may be snow."

She nodded, but said no more.

Soon, there came the sound of hoofbeats, and the faint glow of carriage lanterns could be seen approaching. The groom arrived first, rapidly followed by the magistrate's large carriage. The magistrate, and a burly guard, descended. Hunter went forward to greet them.

"Good evening. My thanks for coming so promptly. I am the Duke of Melton, here to support my sister in law, Lady Granville, in her time of loss. Whilst here, I became aware of some nefarious activity being carried out on the property. We have acted to curtail that, and capture the offenders."

"Your Grace." The magistrate bowed. "Tell me more of these offenders, if you would?"

Hunter called Charles over, and, between them, they explained the chain of circumstance that had led them to this moment. Maria stepped quietly forward as they spoke and stood between them. The magistrate threw her a curious glance, nodded respectfully, and went back to listening. At the mention of the Dowager's words at the funeral (necessary to explain why Charles had connected the idea of highwaymen with the activity at the Dower House), he turned to Maria and bowed.

"My Lady, may I say that neither I, nor anyone I know, put any credence whatsoever in those terrible words? Those in the district who have met you have had only good to say... well, apart from the two who spoke against you at the funeral, and I must attribute that to the effects of overwhelming grief."

Maria acknowledge his words with a gracious nod.

"Thank you. Your words are very much appreciated."

The magistrate turned back to Hunter.

"Forgive me, Your Grace, but I simply had to let Lady Granville know that she is respected. Do go on."

"There is nothing to forgive – indeed, I am grateful for your words. Lady Granville needs all the support possible at this difficult time."

The conversation continued, and when the tale had been told in its whole, the two highway men were brought forward. They sneered angrily at everyone, and refused to answer any question asked by the magistrate. He sighed, and directed his guard to hold the men, whilst Hunter showed him what they had found in the Dower House. As he walked towards the house, one of the highwaymen snarled to the other, in a harsh undertone.

"I told you it was foolish, wouldn't work, wouldn't stop his Lordship – now look where its brought us! It's all your fault."

The magistrate spun back towards them.

"What did you say? What did you tell him wouldn't work?"

The man who had spoken responded, obviously before he had thought it through, his anger overriding his sense.

"Attempting to dissuade his Lordship from repairing this place... indirectly... forcefully..."

The magistrate looked at Charles for a moment, then turned back to the two bound men, his expression serious. He waited, as if expecting the man to say more. When nothing came, he spoke.

"I believe that I just heard you confess to the crime of conspiracy to injure, or perhaps even murder, a Lord of this realm. Regardless of what you may face for highway robbery, you have just doomed yourself to the gallows. Guard, ensure that these criminals are well bound, and load them into the coach, if you would, whilst I see the evidence of their robberies."

The men wailed and suddenly attempted to escape their bindings, but the guard quickly put an end to that. Maria could not find it in her to pity them – they had, by their actions it seemed, caused Edmund's death. She turned away, suddenly sickened by the sight of them, and went back to sit in the stable.

A few moments later, Charles came to her – she looked up at him, and the warmth in his eyes drove all thought of the chill air from her.

"Come, my Lady, let me escort you home. Hunter and Kevin can deal with anything else that needs to happen here – you need to be out of the cold, and away from all of this."

He offered his hand, and she took it, gratefully, rising from her rough seat. He turned to the groom.

"Please bring our horses. I will escort Lady Granville back to Myniard House. You can inform His Grace of our actions when he returns from inside the Dower House."

The groom bowed, and turned away. They stood in silence, waiting his return with the horses, until Charles turned to her again.

"All will be well, I promise you, no matter how long it takes."

She nodded, somehow believing him, believing that he, if anyone, could magically transform her life.

At that moment, the groom returned, and Maria simply allowed him to assist her to mount, the events of the afternoon suddenly overwhelming her. They rode from the light of the carriage in the courtyard, into the deep dark of the fields and the woods. The moon cast a soft silver light across the land, and her eyes slowly adapted to it,

It was an odd sensation, riding beside Charles through the moonlit woods, as if the world did not exist away from them, as if everything that had happened for the last year was some strange dream, some impossible story. They went slowly, trusting the excellent night sight of the horses, riding side by side. Maria realised, with a start, that she felt utterly safe in that moment, with this man. Seconds after that thought crossed her mind, he reached out, and took her hand. The warmth of his touch was welcome. If this was a dream, let it continue. Each guiding their horses with a single hand, they rode on, their other hands linked, neither speaking, as if words would shatter the spell of the moment.

And so they went, until Myniard House was before them. Reluctantly, she slipped her hand from his, and they rode into the stableyard, everything that was proper, as if those moments in the moonlight had never been.

~~~~~

The following morning, they were all surprised when the Dowager joined them at the breakfast table. Expecting that she would ignore them, as she had for the last week, they were even more surprised when she fixed Maria with a stern gaze, and actually spoke directly to her.

"I have a surprise for you." She laughed at Maria's concerned expression. "Yes, you would do well to look worried, you nasty trollop. But, regardless of your opinion, I require you to be present in the house all morning. It will go badly for you if you are not." She turned to glare at the other men present, just as Lord Chester drew breath to speak. "And I'll thank the rest of you not to interfere, although you are welcome to be present. Any objection to what I have planned will only demonstrate this trollop's guilt even more."

"Be assured, my Lady, that I will be present by my daughter's side, throughout whatever ill-conceived thing you may have set in motion."

"Excellent."

Seemingly pleased with the disturbance that her demands had created, the Dowager turned her attention to her food and ate with an appetite and enthusiasm which no one else in the room felt any longer.

An hour later, with the Dowager again retired to her rooms, they sat in the parlour, wondering what it was that would happen that morning, unable to see any way to do more than wait. Maria took up her embroidery again, wondering if this piece would ever be finished, yet needing something to keep her occupied. She looked up to find Charles watching her. Their eyes met, and her hands stilled, the needle partway through the cloth. There was such care, such warmth, such, dare she think it, love, in his eyes that she felt close to tears. Her thoughts went back to those moments in the conservatory, when he had held her while she cried. She wanted to feel like that again – not the tears, but the sense of being safe, protected, cherished.

He smiled, and gave a little shrug, as if to say that he also could not think of anything to do but wait. Maria gave a tiny nod in return, and forced her attention back to the embroidery in her hands. As it turned out, they did not have long to wait.

Within a half hour, there came the sound of carriage wheels on the gravel, soon followed by the opening of the front door. Some minutes passed, and then the Dowagers voice came from the hall.

"Thank you for coming at such short notice, Dr Fitzpatrick. If you would follow me."

"Of course, my Lady."

The parlour door opened, and the Dowager entered, followed by a distinguished looking man who carried a valise of the type often used by doctors to carry their potions and devices. The Dowager fixed Maria with her harsh glare again, and addressed the room.

"This is Doctor Sir Wilfred Fitzpatrick, a physician of renown. I have called him in to assess the... potions... which you administered to my son. I would have proof of your ill doing to your husband, from a source that no one will dispute. Dr Fitzpatrick, this..." she waved her hand in Maria's direction, "is my late son's wife. It is her potions that I believe caused his death. Demand of her whatever you need for your assessment. I will ensure that she complies."

The bitter cruel edge to the Dowager's voice was enough to make Maria shiver a little with fear, but Charles met her eyes and smiled. She drew herself up and stepped forward, smiling as brightly as she could.

"Good day to you, Dr Fitzpatrick. I am Maria, Lady Granville – how may I assist you? I would have this situation resolved as rapidly as possible. Let me introduce the others present." She motioned each person forward in turn, introducing them. "My brother-in-law, the Duke of Melton, my sister, the Duchess of Melton, my father and mother – Lord and Lady Chester, my brother Lord Kevin Loughbridge and His Grace's brother, Lord Wareham."

The doctor's eyes widened a little at the room full of important personages arrayed before him, but he retained his composure admirably. Maria felt the smallest piece of hopefulness – he appeared a reasonable man of good social standing, and gracious manner – perhaps he was not simply a tool to the Dowager's hand.

Once the doctor had acknowledged everyone, bowing elegantly to the ladies present, he turned back to Maria.

"Perhaps, my Lady, it would be best if you told me a little about what you know of medicines, where you learnt this, and why, and then, perhaps you can show me the area in which you prepare things?"

"Of course. Won't you be seated, Doctor? This may take a little while to tell."

The doctor sat, and everyone settled in, watching curiously. The Dowager paced the edge of the room, apparently unable to simply sit. Maria ignored her, to the best of her ability.

"The story, if I am to tell all of it, begins when I was a child."

Maria glanced at her mother, who looked rather startled at these words.

It was to be expected – Maria was about to reveal things that her mother had never known about.

"Tell me whatever you feel necessary, my Lady."

The doctor appeared almost embarrassed at what he had been asked to do here, and seemed most grateful that she was cooperating, rather than there being a terrible scene.

"I became interested in healing plants, and what could be done with them, as a result of my childhood Nurse. For she always had a posset or a simple to treat my sniffles or scratches. And they worked. Nor did they taste as horrible as the medicines that our physician sometimes provided." Maria blushed a little, realising that her words might be interpreted as criticising physicians, but the doctor simply nodded and waited for her to continue. "I was not a child to like the outdoors," Nerissa's stifled laughter made Maria glance her way for a second, "but I was willing to follow my Nurse to see the plants that she used. Over time, I learnt much. I did not tell my mother, for I feared that she would think it an unladylike interest."

Lady Chester looked somewhat offended at Maria's words, and went as if to speak, but an unexpected glare from her other daughter caused her to subside. After a moment Kevin spoke.

"I say Maria, does that mean it was you who ran off with my botany books? I never could work out where they'd gone."

"Yes, that was me. I'm sorry, but I wanted to learn."

Kevin laughed at her reddened cheeks.

"Well you made better use of them, it seems, than I ever would have."

Maria turned back to the doctor, and went on.

"I had a little shed, near the gardener's cottages, and I learnt how to use the plants. The staff helped me, for they wanted the simples I made for their ill children and families. When I came here, I found it… difficult to adapt. The way that the household operated… was so… different from my previous experience." She glanced at the Dowager, whose expression suggested that, if she said anything more specific about the household situation, then retribution would occur later. "I found myself with a need for something to fill my time, so I began to wander the Park, and the close by lanes, looking for plants, and I appropriated an old cottage near the home farm, and used it to store and prepare my possets. Again, the staff here, once they realised what I was doing, helped when they could, bringing me plants when they discovered them."

"How dare they!"

The Dowager's words cut harshly across the conversation, full of anger. The Doctor looked at her enquiringly

"My Lady?"

She turned away, obviously struggling to rein in her anger.

"Nothing. Do go on. This is most informative so far."

The doctor turned back to Maria, a small frown marring his brow.

"I see – will you show me this cottage?"

"Yes, willingly. When my husband suffered his accident, and then took a terrible fever of the lungs, I did what I could to help him – to soothe so that he could sleep, and breathe easier."

The doctor nodded, waiting for her to continue.

"But nothing could save him. Each time, he would swallow what I gave him, and he would seem better for a short time, but, always, he got worse again. And then, despite my personal objections, the physician attending insisted on bleeding him. He weakened immediately – I am quite certain that it hastened his death."

"I am inclined to agree on that point. My experience, in recent years, suggests that bleeding is not as efficacious as it was once thought to be."

Maria relaxed a little in her seat, relived that the doctor shared her views on the topic. The Dowager, however, had stilled in her pacing, and stood stiffly, her eyes angry upon the doctor she had summoned. It seemed that she was not best pleased with his views. Maria thought a moment, unsure if there was anything else she should tell him, then concluded that there was not.

"That is, I think, all of the story. If you would follow me, I will show you the cottage, and all of my herbs and preparations. I must warn you that the path will be well muddied with the recent snow."

"I believe that I can manage a little mud, my Lady."

Maria nodded, and rose. Everyone followed her as she led the doctor from the room, even the Dowager – it seemed that her curiosity overwhelmed her distaste for the muddied paths outside. No one spoke as they walked through the gardens, and down the paths past the home farm, until they reached the simple cottage.

They stepped inside, and Maria stood to one side, leaving the doctor to examine the contents of the room as he would. The swirl of scents from the hanging dried herbs surrounded her, soothing, reassuring – this was the one place in which she usually had control of everything. As the doctor stepped forward, Charles came to stand beside her. Softly, as if by accident, his fingers brushed her arm. She felt it, as if it was searingly hot, even through her warm clothes. She knew, with absolute certainty, that the touch was no accident – it was intentional, and meant to offer her what support he could, under the view of others' eyes. She glanced at him, smiling, then returned her eyes to the doctor.

The man wandered around, lifting bottles, and unstoppering them, carefully sniffing the contents before resealing them, examining herbs and equipment. Finally, he turned to Maria, a bottle in hand.

"My Lady, if you would, tell me what this is, how it was made, and what it might be used for?"

Maria complied, and he simply nodded, and moved on to another item. So it went for over an hour. Maria felt exhausted by the end of it, yet pleased – he had not mocked her in any way, had not spoken against the properties of the possets and simples she created – he had simply nodded each time, and asked about another item. Finally, he replaced the last bottle in its correct place, and spoke.

"Thank you for your patience. We can now return to the parlour – I am certain that you are all ready to be out of the cold and settle by a warm fire."

The Dowager made as if to speak, then simply nodded.

They filed back out of the cottage, and back to the house, the silence almost oppressive.

At the parlour door, the doctor spoke again.

"My Lady, one last thing – would you show me your late husband's rooms, and any items you might have given him, if any remain?"

"As you wish, doctor."

Maria met Charles' eyes for a moment, as he tensed, and almost moved towards her. She gave a tiny shake of her head, then turned and went to the stairs. The doctor followed, waving everyone else back except Lord Chester and the Dowager, who stood, her obvious impatience barely contained - it was clear that she did not like being directed in her own home.

In Edmund's rooms, everything was exactly as it had been on the day of his death. Maria was relieved – it appeared that the dowager's grief had kept her away, and that none had dared touch the rooms without her orders. Maria went to the dresser and indicated the row of bottles.

"This one for his breathing, this one to lower his fever, and this to help him sleep."

The doctor stood beside her, and lifted each bottle in turn, opening them and sniffing their contents. Finally, he turned to her, his eyes kind.

"I must ask this of you my Lady, as a last confirming thing."

The Dowager watched, and, to Maria's eyes, her expression was hungry, and a little desperate – what did she expect to happen now? Lord Chester stood, glaring at the Dowager.

"Yes?"

"Would you drink from each of these bottles, my Lady?" Maria gasped, understanding the implication of his words. But his eyes were kind, and flicked momentarily towards the Dowager. In that moment, Maria understood his intent – he seemed to bear no ill will towards her, and was seeking a way to absolutely prove his point.

"I will do so, Sir, right now, if you wish it."

"I would be grateful if you would, my Lady."

Maria took each bottle in turn, uncorked it, and took a sizeable swallow – less so from the sleeping draught than the others, as sleep would not be helpful now. Then she turned to face the Dowager, and, for the first time since this ridiculous activity had commenced, spoke directly to her.

"Are you satisfied now, my Lady? Has this waste of the good doctor's time convinced you that I did not poison, nor intend to poison, my husband? For I believe that the doctor will confirm my words."

"Indeed I will, Lady Granville, and I thank you for your forbearance as I have conducted this investigation as it was commissioned by the Dowager Countess." He turned to the Dowager, and spoke directly to her, an edge of irritation in his voice. "Lady Granville, I have found not one shred of evidence of any malfeasance on the younger Lady Granville's part. Her knowledge in the area of medicines is excellent – I could wish that many physicians knew as much. Nothing I found in her cottage, or in her herbs and infusions, was of a nature designed to harm. And she has just amply demonstrated that, by taking her own medicine."

The Dowager's face turned an unbecoming shade of crimson.

"I do not believe you sir! Surely, there is something there which is beyond the acceptable?"

"There is not. Now let us return to your parlour – I feel it only fair that I declare my findings in this matter before everyone present."

The Dowager went to speak again, full of blustering anger, but Lord Chester stepped forward.

"I will thank you to stop maligning my daughter, my Lady. It is time to see this farce ended – let us do as the good doctor suggests, and repair to the parlour."

The Dowager glared, but could not find a reason to refuse the suggestion. They returned to the lower floor in silence.

~~~~

Charles paced about the parlour, unable to be still, wishing desperately that he had reason to have gone upstairs with Maria. At least her father, true to his word, was with her. For whilst the physician had behaved with great courtesy so far, Charles still did not trust what he might do – after all, he was present at the Dowager's behest.

There came a knock at the door, and everyone turned – it was too soon for Maria and the others to have returned – and the Dowager would certainly not have knocked. Moments later, Thompson, looking concerned, ushered the magistrate into the room.

"My Lords and Ladies, Your Grace, I trust you are well today? Might I have a little of your time, to confirm some of the details again, before the highwaymen are finally dealt with?"

Hunter stepped forward.

"Certainly, how can we help?"

"I simply need to hear the details of how you identified the men, and located their hiding place, again. I must inform you that you were also correct about them using the old tower on Lady Fremont's property – our search there uncovered a very large amount of stolen goods – many were identifiable pieces of jewellery, which had been reported as stolen in highway robberies."

"I am glad that so many goods have been recovered, and will be, I hope, returned to their owners. But come, sit, and we will call for tea, then we can go through the whole story again for you."

"My thanks, Your Grace."

Once the tea had been delivered, they told the tale again, in even greater detail than the night before, noting how it all tied together with the Dowager's accusations of Maria, and the somewhat unusual circumstances of Lord Granville's accident, which led to his death. Charles also explained that the Dowager still persisted in her condemnation of Maria – to the extent that a learned physician was, at that moment, 'investigating' Maria's medicines. The magistrate looked most shocked.

"Your Grace, I do not understand how the Dowager can believe ill of Lady Granville – her possets have helped half the village!"

"Nonetheless, the Dowager Countess appears utterly convinced of Lady Granville's ill intent."

The magistrate shook his head, muttering quietly.

"Shocking. Most shocking!"

He did not have the chance to say more, for at that moment the door opened.

~~~~

Downstairs, the parlour was quiet. All eyes turned to Maria and her companions as they entered, and she realised that there was an extra person present – the magistrate. More to witness her humiliation, she thought, wryly. Well, it was no worse than she had suffered throughout her marriage. The doctor stepped forward.

"I have completed my assessment of Lady Granville's herbal preparations, as I was commissioned to do. I will now deliver my opinion on the matter, before all present, that there might be no doubt of my words. I have found nothing whatsoever in any of Lady Granville's herbs or preparations, to indicate any intent to harm, or, indeed, the production of any potion capable of harm. In addition, to confirm my assessment, I asked lady Granville to drink from each of the bottles which contained potions which she had administered to her late husband. She did so without hesitation. I thank her for her forbearance as I have done what I was commissioned to do. A set of actions which, I believe, were entirely unnecessary."

The Dowager glared at the man.

Lady Chester looked at her husband, who nodded, confirming what had happened.

"Thank you, doctor, for your courtesy in dealing with this. Might we all now return to the other matters in our day?"

"Certainly, I have no need to further disturb you."

He bowed to all, and last to the Dowager, then left the room. The Dowager, freed by his exit, scowled at everyone, then focussed on the magistrate.

"And what are you doing here? As the good doctor has not succeeded in providing information adequate for me to suggest that you lock up this hussy for murder, I do not understand your presence in my home."

The magistrate drew himself up, and appeared to consciously choose to ignore her rudeness.

"My Lady, I am here to consult with your guests, who, last night, were successful in bringing to justice the highwaymen who have plagued the roads between here and London for months. The reprobates were, it seems, also responsible for Lord Granville's 'accident', and therefore his death. They were using your Dower House to store their stolen goods, and when Lord Granville began the work to restore the building, they decided to act to stop him."

The Dowager paled at his words and collapsed into the nearest chair. To Maria, her next words seemed illogical, and out of place.

"He was... restoring the Dower House...?"

"Yes, my Lady."

"No... he wouldn't have dared, he couldn't have intended... no." She turned to Maria, her eyes filled with hate and accusation. "It's all your fault, if you had never married him, he would never have thought to do that, to plan to cast me from my own home into that old ruin. And if the magistrate speaks the truth, had you not planted that idea in his head, he would still be alive today. It's as if you had murdered him, even if the good doctor says you did not do so directly. You're a scheming immoral woman, I know that you wanted my son dead, so that you could run off with a lover, I'm sure of it, and nothing will change my mind!"

There was a moment's shocked silence in the room, then Lord Chester moved to stand directly before the Dowager. When he spoke, his voice was low, and threatening. Maria had never before heard her father sound dangerous, but at that moment he did.

"My Lady, you are overwrought. I will not permit you to speak to my daughter that way. The doctor who you called in has cleared her of all wrongdoing, and it is also clear that no-one other than your son knew of the work at the Dower House – for my daughter has that in your son's hand – a letter received after his death, telling of his plans for the Dower House – which was the first that my daughter knew of it. I suggest that you retire to your rooms and compose yourself."

He turned, and rang the bell. When Thompson appeared, Lord Chester indicated the Dowager where she sat, almost spluttering, as she tried to compose a response to his words.

"Lady Granville is overcome. Please summon her maid to help her to her rooms immediately."

Thompson nodded, and left the room.

"You can't order me…"

"Yes, I can and will, when you behave so inappropriately." The maid appeared in the doorway. "Please assist your mistress to her rooms – she is overwrought."

The maid looked at Lord Chester's stern face, then at the angry Dowager and went to her, nervously. The Dowager snarled at her when she touched her arm.

"Do not argue, my Lady, lest I find it necessary to escort you to your rooms forcibly."

Suddenly, the Dowager's face crumpled, the anger fading to confused misery. She stifled a sob, then let the maid lead her from the room.

"Thank you, Father. I think that is the first time that anyone has truly defied and directed her in her life. And that is, in my opinion, a long overdue event."

Chapter Fourteen

Within a few days, the magistrate had prepared all of the required paperwork, and was ready to send the highwaymen to their fate. Given the cloud which had been cast over Maria's name, he chose to make their official sentencing public. Maria was nervous as she stood, surrounded by her family and friends, in the town square, to see it done. She drew strength from the fact that Charles stood close by, from the care with which he had assisted her down from the carriage, and from the look in his eyes when their eyes met.

The square was full of people, all curious, muttering and gawking at Maria while they waited for the event of the day to begin. Maria felt rather as she imagined an animal in a menagerie must – and it was not at all pleasant. Finally, the magistrate emerged from his office, the two men bound and hauled along behind him by two guards. A hushed whisper of conversation went through the crowd.

The magistrate made a great show of positioning the men where everyone could see them.

He produced a large sheet of paper, and began to read.

"All present bear witness to the fact that these two men, Peter Timms and Bob Abbott, have been found guilty of multiple crimes, to whit, highway robbery and conspiracy to injure or kill a Lord of this land. They intentionally set out to harm Lord Granville, by firing a dart or arrow at his horse in a situation where he was almost certain to be injured. His resulting fall into the river led to his illness and death. For these crimes, they are sentenced to the gallows, and will be sent to Newgate immediately, there to wait the hangman's pleasure."

Gasps went through the crowd, and Maria could see the biggest gossips in the district looking between her, and the magistrate, edging closer all the while. The magistrate went to speak again, but a sharp voice rose above the crowd – Lucy Morton thrust herself forward.

"That's all very well, if they caused him to fall, but what of the witch, with her potions? Surely it was her who caused his actual death!"

The magistrate drew himself up and raised his voice over the loud mutterings of the crowd.

"Silence! You will cease this disrespectful accusation at once. Sir Wilfred Fitzpatrick, a learned and highly regarded physician from London, came and assessed all of Lady Granville's herbs and potions, including those in the actual bottles used to treat Lord Granville, and declared them all wholesome and helpful. Lady Granville is innocent of all wrongdoing, and I will thank you to remember that."

The muttering subsided a little, and Lucy Morton stepped back, suddenly unsure of support.

"I would suggest that you all focus on being glad that your roads are safer, with these men brought to justice, rather than on insulting Lady Granville with your gossip."

Hunter's voice was harsh, and the townspeople close to him fell back a little. Then they all turned back to the magistrate as he spoke again.

"My guards will escort these men, ensuring that they cannot escape to trouble the King's roads again. Now that you have seen justice done, disperse, return to your homes and do not indulge in idle gossip."

The crowd stood and watched the bound men loaded into a carriage, and only moved off once it was gone on its way. Maria and her family took advantage of their distraction to slip away, glad to know that the highwaymen were dealt with. Whether the townspeople would listen to the magistrate's words was another matter.

Once back at Myniard House, Maria collapsed onto a couch in the parlour, suddenly overcome with tiredness. Her mother looked at her with concern, and rang for tea. When it arrived, Charles brought her a cup, urging her to drink. She smiled at him gratefully, suddenly wishing that she could throw herself into his arms, could feel safe, could cry, and release all of the fear and stress of the last few months. But she could not. Propriety must be observed. She sipped the tea, hoping that her eyes told him how much she appreciated his care. All was quiet, until dinner. They spent the afternoon discussing what should happen next, and, although a little unsure of whether it was too soon, and she might still be seen as running away, Maria eventually agreed that she should return to her parents' home.

Once the decision was made, Maria wanted nothing more than to be gone from Myniard House as soon as possible. They settled on leaving the following day, for all would need time to pack, and another carriage would need to be hired, to carry all of Maria's possessions.

They went in to dinner with everyone feeling happier than they had for weeks. Once they were all seated, Charles reached for Maria's hand beneath the table, gently squeezing her fingers, she smiled at him, and returned the pressure, before removing her hand. Unexpectedly, the Dowager entered the room. They had expected her to keep to her rooms, as she had since the doctor's visit.

She sat, and looked around the table before meeting Maria's eyes. Her smile was not a pleasant sight, and her voice, when she spoke, was sharp and bitter.

"I hear that you made a spectacle of yourself in the town this afternoon. Just what I might have expected from a trollop like you. Will you never be finished with bringing disgrace to my family name?"

Maria looked at her in amazement – how had she heard anything of the day's events? And how could she interpret things the way that she had? Anger rushed through Maria – anger for everything that this woman had done to her for the last year, and boiled over – she would be gone from here tomorrow, there was no reason now, to hold back.

"Obviously, someone has reported to you a distorted version of events. And, typical of you, you believe your gossiping cronies and their evil words more than anything I could tell you."

The Dowager spluttered with rage, but Maria went on, the words pouring forth unstoppably.

"The truth of it, whether you believe it or not, is that I watched as the magistrate sentenced the highwaymen to hang, before the whole town. And then, when your 'old friend' Lucy Morton accused me of being a witch and a poisoner, the magistrate told everyone about the findings of 'your' doctor, and declared me unequivocally innocent of wrongdoing. If anyone brought public attention and scandal to your name, it was Lucy Morton, by creating a scene in the first place. You are a cruel, bitter old woman, you controlled and limited your son all of his life. If you had done what is expected of a woman in your position in society, and moved to the Dower House when your son married, he would still be alive today – none of this would have happened."

"I... how dare you!"

"Easily – I am past caring about you, and your nastiness, I wish you well of it, for the rest of your lonely life. I have no intention of staying here so that you can abuse me as you have since I arrived. Tomorrow I will remove myself from this place, and return to my parents' house. I will take only what is mine, according to the terms of our marriage contract, and I will be glad never to return here."

The Dowager's face had reddened with intense anger, and she scanned the faces around her, seeing no sympathy anywhere.

"Good riddance, I say, to all of you. I will be glad to see the back of you, you, who have destroyed my life with your meddling ways. I find my appetite is gone."

So saying, the Dowager stood, and stormed from the room. Silence followed for some minutes.

"Well said, sister, I believe that she deserved every word. In fact, I think that you were far more restrained in your words than I might have been in your situation."

Hunter laughed at Nerissa's words.

"Yes, I suspect that you would have been far less restrained, my ferocious Duchess!"

Everyone laughed a little too, and the tension was broken. Maria flushed, suddenly embarrassed at having been more forthright than she had ever been before in her life.

~~~~~

By midday of the next day, a cavalcade of carriages stood ready on the drive of Myniard House. Charles was ahorse beside them, his eyes on Maria as she settled onto the carriage seat.

"I will see you in a month or two, once I have been to the estates that I have neglected these last many weeks. Travel well, and may your life, Lady Granville, even whilst in mourning, be far more pleasant from now on."

He bowed to her from his relaxed seat on the horse, and she looked up at him, her eyes shining with something he desperately hoped was affection, or more than simple affection.

"Thank you, my Lord, I will look forward to your company on your return."

The warmth of her voice heated him through.

The carriage door was closed, and he turned away, riding in the opposite direction to the carriages, from the end of the drive. He had much work to do, and not just in attending to Hunter's estates – he still had not found Marion, and his failure in his promise to Martin burned his soul. But he felt a terrible pull – part of him wanted nothing more than to turn, and ride after the carriages, to be by Maria's side, always, to hold her and help her as she found her way through the mourning period and back into her life.

He pushed the feeling aside – he could do nothing, could not even consider speaking to her of his feelings, until more than six months of her mourning was done. To do so would bring more scandal down upon her – even after six months, he would need to be circumspect. He would never do anything to hurt her, so his choice was obvious – attend to his duties, and allow them to keep him away for much of the time, so that he was never tempted to be inappropriate.

It would be a long year, but somehow, he would manage, and still see Maria whenever he appropriately could.

~~~~~

When the carriages finally split into two groups, hers turning into the gates of Chester Park and the others going to Meltonbrook Chase, a short distance further on, Maria finally felt as if there was hope, as if the fact that she would never have to return to Myniard House was real. She looked eagerly out of the carriage window as the familiar house came into sight, and, when Kevin reached out and patted her hand, she was close to tears.

"Welcome home, Maria."

The tears overflowed, and she crumpled against her mother's shoulder. Lady Chester patted her back soothingly, and held her until the carriage drew up in front of the house.

The next few hours were a pleasant chaos of explaining to the staff, seeing to the unloading of the carriages and the disposition of everyone's possessions, and settling in to her room again – a room that she had thought she'd left forever. It seemed smaller somehow, different, yet warm and friendly, and safe. But the thought of safety brought her mind back to those minutes in the conservatory at Myniard House, when Charles had held her as she cried. This kind of safe was good, but, she admitted to herself, being held by Charles was better. Would she ever feel his arms around her again? She did not know – but she knew that she wanted to, very, very much.

The weeks flowed by, and Charles had not returned to Meltonbrook Chase. Maria slowly relaxed, and became less gaunt, less tired, and less fearful. She walked through the Park, and through the Meltonbrook grounds as well, taking pleasure in the outdoors in a way that she never had before. Having the freedom to do as she pleased was wonderful, and she valued every day. Nerissa was amused, for she had never been able to convince Maria to spend much time outdoors when they were children, but she was glad that Maria was doing something, rather than sitting and being miserable.

Hunter and Nerissa were away for a while, attending Hunter's friend, Viscount Pendholm's wedding, and Maria found that she missed her sister, for the first time in her life. But she missed Charles more. She never spoke of him, but he was in her thoughts often.

∿∿∿∿∿

Charles had stayed away from Meltonbrook Chase far longer than he had intended. Somehow, whilst he longed to see Maria, he could not bear the thought of doing so, and needing to stay formal, and somewhat distant. The estates, and his search for Marion, made an excellent excuse to stay away. He did not go, although he was invited, to either Viscount Pendholm's or Lord Geoffrey Clarence's weddings – he simply could not bear the thought of watching others happy and able to marry the ones they loved. Call him a coward, but work was easier.

Still, whilst Hunter's estates flourished, with the spring and early summer far warmer than the previous year, his search for Marion still floundered. He was beginning to think that he would have to tell Martin's father of it, and beg his help. Perhaps he should have done that long before, but his pride had held him back, as had his concern that Martin's mother would react badly. But the Duchess of Windemere was now more than a year in her grave, and perhaps he should swallow his pride, and do the right thing for his friend's memory.

He would go back to Meltonbrook Chase for some weeks first, and allow himself the privilege of seeing Maria, perhaps of walking or riding with her. And he would discover if she felt for him as he felt for her, or if he had imagined her responses, when she had been so distressed and in difficult conditions.

∿∿∿∿∿

May had arrived, and with it a vast array of flowers.

Maria was out walking, collecting flowers and plants to begin making remedies again, when, in the distance, she saw the shape of a rider on the road. She knew him instantly. Her heart beat faster. Would he still want to see her? Had she imagined what she had seen in his eyes, back at Myniard House, when he had saved her from the highwayman? She could not know – but, no matter what, she had to see him, and soon. She could not bear to be so close and not see him. he had been back once before, but only for a short while, as arrangements happened for his sister Sybilla's wedding. She had not seen him at all that time, and had worried that perhaps he avoided her.

She gathered up her basket full of plants and flowers, and continued on her way, barely aware of the world around her, whilst her mind relived every moment in which he had ever shown her care. When she reached the gardeners' shed she used here for her preparations, she found herself simply standing at the table, lost in thought. Finally, giving up on getting anything useful done, and with no sense of how much time had passed while she stood there, she simply laid out or hung the plants and flowers to dry, and returned to the house.

Not long after, as she sat in the parlour reading, there came a knock at the front door. Footsteps sounded on the hall floor, then Ward tapped and opened the parlour door, ushering the visitor in.

"Viscount Wareham, my Lady."

Maria rose, and simply stood, drinking in the sight of him. He was as handsome as ever, his dark hair a little longer, a lock falling over his forehead where the wind of travel had disarrayed it. His hazel eyes met hers, and the world faded away from around her.

Warmth flooded her body, and her breath came faster. She felt unable to move, unable to speak, yet she wanted to fling herself at him, to feel his arms around her.

Ward shut the door, and the faint click as it shut remained the only sound in the room. They stood, eyes locked together, for long minutes. Somewhere in the depths of her mind, she knew that she was being rude, she should greet him, yet she could not break the spell. Finally, she managed to drag her eyes away, to remember to breathe, and to gather her manners together.

"Welcome, my Lord. It is good to see you again after so long. Shall I ring for tea and biscuits?"

"My Lady, it is good to see you, too. And yes, tea would be most welcome, thank you."

She rang the bell, and requested tea, then settled back onto the couch and, greatly daring, waved him to the seat beside her. He sat, and the warmth of his presence, so close beside her seemed greater than should be possible. Her heart beat faster, and she licked her lips, nervously. She looked up at him, to find his eyes following the movement of her tongue, and she flushed, feeling her cheeks heat to an undoubtedly unbecoming red. The silence lengthened. Oh! This was ridiculous! She had always been adept in social situations – why could she not simply talk to this man? Although... the intimacy of them being alone together in the room was disconcerting – she had still not adapted to the change in circumstances, the different rules which governed a widow's life, as compared to those that constrained an unmarried, or a married, lady. She searched for something to say, resorting to the boring aspects of daily life, when no other ideas came.

"You find me alone, my Lord – my father is about estate business, my mother has gone to visit her cousin, and my brother has gone to London for a week or two."

"I assure you, my Lady, that your company will be more than enough."

"I…" She was not certain of what she had intended to say, and was relieved when the maid brought in the tea tray, necessitating that she turned her attention to that. Once the maid was gone, and she had drawn out the process of pouring the tea, she had regained her composure. How did he discompose her so easily? "You are gracious, my Lord – I shall try not to disappoint." She set her teacup down on the table, and watched as he did the same. As if in a dream, she watched as his hand reached for hers. The heat of his touch spread through her.

"My Lady… Maria… you could never disappoint me, never. I am glad that we have this moment alone. I came because I needed… needed to see you, to know that you are well, that the terrible events of your marriage and your husband's death have done no lasting harm. You look much improved – to me, you are always beautiful, but now, there is a lightness about you, compared to those dark days. It is good to see you so."

"My Lord… Charles…" she blushed again, the sound of his name on her own lips emphasising the intimacy of the moment, "you are too kind – for I know that, by the time of Edmund's death, I was far from beautiful. I hope that these last months of rest have helped my appearance somewhat. But they have helped my heart more. I no longer blame myself for not loving my husband."

She looked down, her eyes falling upon their joined hands. Somehow, with this man, although he discomposed her, and caused all ability at polite conversation to disappear, at the same time, he was someone she could speak to of the most personal matters, without hesitation. It confused her.

"That is good. For in not loving him, yours was no different from most society marriages, after all."

"True. But... I believe that I am coming to understand what love is like. Is it wrong of me, when I am still in mourning, to think of such things?" Her eyes met his again, and she saw a moment of doubt. She shook her head, lifted her free hand, and softly touched his face. "Do not look so concerned, Charles. I was not clear in my meaning – I am not... experienced... at talking about these things. But... I meant..." She felt her cheeks redden again, but he had stilled at her touch, and his gaze devoured her, full of hope and fear. "I meant, Charles, that it is you who have made me begin to understand love. Am I too forward? Am I a fool, who misinterprets things? Or... do you, perhaps, care for me?"

She was instantly overcome by fear – what had she done? What if she was wrong, what if his care was nothing beyond that of a good friend and neighbour? She waited, her life hanging on the thread of his next words. He tensed beneath her touch, and his fingers tightened on hers. Then, so slowly it seemed, his free hand reached up and cupped the curve of her neck, drawing her to him. His lips met hers, softly, exploring, in a kiss that rapidly became something deeper, hungry, an expression of months of uncertainty, of desire and of hopeful love. She melted into it, her heart singing at his actions, a strange tightness filling her body.

When they finally drew apart, he smiled, his eyes full of that same love she had seen in the moments when he had saved her from the highwayman.

"Maria… I have always loved you – since we were children. I see nothing wrong with you considering love now, even when your mourning year is not finished. But I know that society might see things differently. I would not bring the faintest touch of scandal to your name – especially not after what you have been through. That's why I have stayed away so long. I wanted to see you, but I could not bear…"

"Oh Charles! I never thought I'd say this, but there are times when I think that the ways of society are very wrong. But you are right, they might well condemn me., if I allowed my feelings for you to be visible, before my mourning ends. Can you… can you wait for me? Can we manage to talk, to see each other, over this next six months and more, and still appear the picture of propriety?"

"Maria, my darling… I can do anything, anything that you need, if I know that there is hope, that when your mourning is finished, we might spend time together, might see if we want to spend our lives together…"

Tears sprang to her eyes, and he gathered her to him, holding her close, safe. She never wanted to move from his arms again, but, eventually, she pulled away, and straightened her skirts where they had crushed against him.

"Charles, I want that, so very much. But if we must wait all of those months, we had best begin now, the way that we must go on – with propriety and distance. For, I fear that, unless I hold myself back, I might betray my feelings constantly."

"I think that we both feel that way. To not touch you, not even your hand, will be hard, when I would hold you, and keep you safe from ever suffering again, if I had the chance, but I will manage. And, I will still need to be away, regularly, for Hunter's estate business, which will make it both easier and harder."

"It will. But simply knowing… knowing how you feel – that will be enough, when I cannot see you."

He lifted her hand to his lips, turning it to place a gentle kiss upon her palm, and nodded.

"Let us begin, then, by talking of everything but us. Tell me about your family, and all that has happened here, since your return from Myniard House."

Maria curled her hand tightly, as if holding the warmth of his kiss tight, and smiled, though her heart felt sore at the need to pretend, to keep distance between them. She spoke of how strange it was to be back here, when she had not expected to return, of how her mother treated her differently, now seeing her with clearer sight, after all of the revelations at Myniard House, and of how Kevin was even more protective than ever, as if he felt that the whole world threatened her.

Charles laughed at her descriptions, and then told her of the things he had seen on various of Hunter's estates, of the investments that might be made and the improvements, of the ideas he had for the future. He spoke of the woollen mill he hoped to establish on one estate, and the potential for change in agriculture. Maria found herself fascinated by things that she had never really thought about in depth before. Perhaps her mother was right, and she was different now. The afternoon slid towards evening, and still they talked.

It was as if the ordinary words hid another conversation entirely, one said with looks, and smiles, which spoke to their feelings, and their hopes for the future, whilst their actual words simply dealt with the practical and ordinary parts of life.

Eventually, as Charles rose to take his leave, Lord Chester returned. He looked a little surprised to find Charles in his parlour, but greeted him cheerfully.

"Wareham – good to see you back. All is well with the Melton estates, I hope?"

"It is, my Lord. I'll not be here for too long though – I'm off to London next, and the round of managing the estates is never really done."

"Too true, too true. Mine keep me busy, and I've nothing on the scale of yours."

"If you'll excuse me, I'll be on my way, my Lord. I came to see how everyone was, now that the unpleasantness at Myniard House is well behind you. I'm pleased to see that Lady Granville is looking far more happy, and you seem well, my Lord."

"Indeed, all bad business that. But it's behind us now. I hope I'll see you again before you leave for London?"

"Of a certainty, my Lord."

Charles bowed, and departed. Maria watched him go, wanting, with all her heart, that he could stay. Then she shook her head a little, and steeled herself to the months of patient waiting before her. Her father watched her, a small smile on his face.

"Fine young man, that one. Does an excellent job of managing his brother's estates."

"Yes. He is both astute and honourable."

"And did you have a pleasant conversation with him?"

Maria looked at her father, curious suddenly, about the turn of his questions.

"Yes, I did. He told me of the plans he has to improve the Melton estates. It was surprisingly fascinating."

"Good, good."

Her father took himself off to his study, leaving Maria bemused, and wondering what that had been about.

~~~~~

For Charles, the next few months rushed by, for, when he sought out the Duke of Windemere to lay before him his failure in the matter of his son's dying wish, a series of events led to Marion finally being found. The Dowager Lady Pendholm was involved, and, much to Charles' delight, in that few short months a match was made between her, and the Duke – a far better match for both of them than their first marriages had been.

He managed to visit Meltonbrook Chase a number of times, and always spent time with Maria, walking in the grounds, or simply sitting and talking. Very cautious at first, over time, he allowed his deep love for her to be more visible to her family, and was pleased when her father appeared happy with him.

For Maria, the time went much slower – she felt suspended in a place detached from the flow of life, waiting for her mourning year to end. Charles' visits were the joy in her life.

By October, she was bored, completely, although her stocks of medicines were large, for that is where she had focussed all of her energy. When the invitation came for her family to attend the Dowager Lady Pendholm's wedding to the Duke of Windemere, Maria looked to her mother with hope.

"My year of mourning is more than half done – surely, if I dress suitably, and do not dance, it would be permissible to attend a wedding? I would love to see other people, to see another place – much as I love Chester Park, I am bored."

Lady Chester considered a moment, then nodded.

"You have the right of it – I see no difficulty in what you suggest. It is time that we started to look to what you will do, once your mourning is over."

"Thank you!"

She spent the following days in a happy daze, especially once she became aware of the fact that Charles would also be at the wedding. She began to feel, just a little, truly alive again.

Chapter Fifteen

At the wedding, Maria behaved as was required, dressed in a sober mourning gown of a dark purply grey. Not quite black, in recognition of the fact that the first six months of her mourning were done, but still an absolute commitment to propriety and society's expectations. She stood quietly to the side at the wedding breakfast and the Ball that followed, watching others dance.

At one point, Charles came to stand beside her.

"I wish so that my mourning was over. I would love to dance again." Maria's voice was soft and sad.

"It will not be much longer. I promise that there will be dancing, as soon as it can possibly be."

The look they exchanged said much, and no further words seemed necessary. But for Maria, those words from him were a promise – a promise about the life they might make, once her mourning was done, and she could leave all trace of her ill-fated marriage to Lord Granville behind.

Somehow, those words, then, made the next three months easier, as the end of her mourning approached. Charles visited often, and Maria came to believe that her father approved, although he said nothing, and her mother simply smiled, and left them alone. The possibility of happiness began to seem closer, and the cold of the winter snows did nothing to dim her mood.

When Christmas arrived, she felt a sense of unreality in the day, remembering the previous year at Myniard House, with Edmund deathly ill, and no joy in anyone's life. The contrast was astounding. Here, she was surrounded by people who were happy in their lives, where neighbours came to visit because they liked each other, and where the servants were well treated, and given good food and gifts for their families for the Christmas season.

In a few short weeks, she might cast off her dark colours, and wear the bright shades she had always so loved. And then... then, she might cautiously admit to having an affection for Charles, and they might, perhaps, let the world see that they cared. But not too soon – after her life with the Dowager Countess she found herself with a great fear of public disapprobation. Still, she counted the days until the anniversary of Edmund's death.

~~~~~

For Charles, things slowed as Christmas approached – the estates were all well prepared for winter, and, with Marion found and happily cared for by Martin's father, there was little that demanded his attention, for the first time in four years.

He allowed himself to see Maria more, and their conversation often turned to his plans for woollen mills, and for other improvements on the more northern estates. She seemed genuinely interested, and he began to imagine a life with her – a life with Seasons in London, but most of the year spent on a pleasant country estate, where they might simply be themselves. Perhaps it was foolish to dream, but he could not help himself. He watched with delight as Maria began to brighten with every day that brought the anniversary of her husband's death closer.

He also, in those weeks around Christmas, found himself spending more and more time with Maria's father and brother, who seemed to have, without a word said, begun to treat him as if he were a part of their family. The day before Christmas, as he rode out in the crisp winter air with Kevin, simply because both of them were tired of being cooped up inside, Kevin turned to him, smiling, and spoke.

"I've been meaning to say something, and this seems a suitable time."

"Say something?"

"Yes – about Maria. You care for her, don't you? And I suspect that she cares for you. I approve. And, most importantly, so do my parents. They don't discuss it much, but every so often, Father will make a comment which makes it clear to me that he likes you, approves of you. He'll wait for you to talk to him, of course, but I think he's happy."

"Thank you. Yes, we care for each other. And I've been worried about what your father thinks, although he's always courteous to me."

Kevin laughed with genuine amusement.

"Father can be gruff, but I get the impression that he's mellowed rather a lot lately, especially since Hunter turned out so well, and Nerissa is so happy. I'd say that he's no idea of how to raise the subject with you – so of course he'll make you start the conversation."

"I see. Well then, I'll just have to pick my time, won't I?"

"Yes – shouldn't be too hard."

They rode on, and Charles thought about Kevin's words, his heart filled with happiness – if Maria's family already approved... the next few weeks could not pass quickly enough.

~~~~~

The day of the anniversary of Edmund's death dawned clear and bright, the sun shining on a new fall of snow. Maria rose from her bed, folded a wrap around her, and went to the window. Outside, the world was white, pristine, the snow untrammelled, untouched, and the ice sparkling as it melted from the trees.

It was as if a hand had washed the world clean, painted it white, a new canvas to draw her life upon, from that moment forward. She sighed, filled with an odd melancholy – joy, and yet sadness. This was a point of enormous change in her life. Today, her last obligation to Edmund was done. All that remained of her marriage to him was the name and title she now bore. And, perhaps, if she let herself hope, that too might soon be gone from her, if she should be so fortunate as to marry again.

There was a tap at the door, and Annie, who had come with her from Myniard House, came in, carrying a jug of hot water for her washbasin.

"Oh, you're up! I'll just put this here and stir up the fire – you don't want to be getting a chill!"

"Thank you, Annie. I didn't even think of it, didn't notice the cold. Because..."

"Because today, everything changes. Doesn't it, my Lady? What gown would you like to wear today, my Lady? I've made sure that all of your bright and beautiful gowns are clean and in good repair."

Maria felt close to tears at the thought of wearing colours again, and was grateful for Annie's forethought. But the maid had good reason to care for her well – Maria had been her path to escape from a miserable life at Myniard House, and Annie would never forget that fact.

"I, don't know. Suddenly, there is too much choice, after so long without needing to think of such things. Something bright, please, perhaps a soft green or a blue?"

Annie went into the dressing room, as Maria rinsed her hands and face in the warm water that Annie had brought. Soon, she returned, bearing a pale green gown which Maria had worn only once before. It was beautiful, of a fine light wool – warm, but soft and flowing.

"This, my Lady?"

"Oh yes, Annie, that will do wonderfully!"

"Very well, my Lady, we'll have you ready in a trice."

Half an hour later, as Maria sat at breakfast, the world still seemed bright and wonderful. As each member of the family came in, they exclaimed about how good it was to see her in colours again, how beautiful she looked. She thought that, perhaps, they exaggerated, but she was grateful for their words, nonetheless.

The day drifted by in a dreamlike way, and Maria felt as if a weight had been lifted from her, as if she was floating. By early afternoon, as she sat in the parlour with a book, it was beginning to feel almost real. Then there came a knock at the door, and Ward showed Charles into the room. Lady Chester rose to greet him, smiling broadly.

"Lord Wareham, how kind of you to call. I'll leave you with Maria – I must go and discuss the week's menus with Cook."

"Thank you, Lady Chester."

Maria stood were she was, having risen from her seat upon his arrival, drinking in his presence. On what was already a wonderful day, having him here made it perfect. He turned, as her mother left the room, and saw her. He stilled, his eyes going wide. She could see, again, in his expression, the love that she had seen there before. And today, she could begin to explore that, today, she was free.

She stepped forward, and into his arms.

~~~~~

Charles had woken early, and his first thought was of Maria. This was the day. The day that they had both been waiting for.

He'd wanted to rush straight to Chester Park, to see her, but had restrained himself until a socially polite hour of the day. Upon his arrival at Chester Park, he had been shown into the house as always, and greeted cheerfully by Lady Chester, who had, as so often of late, immediately left him alone with Maria.

He'd turned to greet her, and completely lost his ability to speak. She was stunningly beautiful, her gown a soft green that somehow made her eyes seem brighter, her hair glowing golden and lit with sparks of red that made it seem fiery, where the sun from the window caught it. It was as if he had never seen her before, never known the reality of her beauty, so strong was the impact upon him.

He had loved her for more than half of his life, today was the day on which he might dare hope to act on that love, and have it reciprocated. Her eyes met his, and were filled with such love, such warmth and joy, that his heart beat faster and his mouth went dry. Automatically, without any thought involved, his hands went out towards her. It was all the encouragement she needed. She stepped forward, fast, as if he might disappear if she delayed, and arrived in his arms. He wrapped her round, cradling her against him, treasuring the feeling, the scent of her, the joy of touching her.

They stood, arms wrapped around each other, simply breathing, both hearts racing in time. When she finally lifted her head, it was the most natural thing in the world to lower his lips to hers, to say with his kiss so much more than could be said with words. They stayed that way, lost in each other, for long minutes, until she pulled away a little, sighing. He waiting, sensing that she would speak, that she searched for words.

"I would stay like this forever, if I could. But I can't, we can't, not yet. But today, we can begin, we can make the first small moves towards something more."

"Yes. Maria, you are so very beautiful - to see you in colour, to know that you are finally free… I have dreamed of this day. But we will do this as you wish it, when you are ready. I want no scandal or distress of any kind to mar your life, to mar what we can have, together."

"Charles… I… I am afraid. I know that's silly of me, but, after the Dowager, after what happened at Myniard House… I am terrified of standing before society, and having everyone condemn me… I would not give them any excuse to decide that I have moved too fast, have done anything of which they might disapprove. So… will you spend time with me, but circumspectly? Carefully, so that we do not let the world see our feelings, until some more time has passed?"

"Maria, my darling Maria, I will do whatever you wish, so long as I can spend some time with you. I would delight in taking you driving about the countryside, but if that makes you feel too exposed, then I will simply come here, where we can sit and talk, or walk in the gardens and the Park, away from other prying eyes."

"Thank you! oh thank you!"

Charles was rocked on his feet as she flung her arms around him again, and he held her tightly to him, feeling the shape of his future, in her form.

∿∿∿∿

A week later, Charles left again, to see to one of Hunter's estates, promising to be back soon, leaving Maria feeling disconsolate, and lonely. She laughed at herself a little, for nothing had really changed, compared to the months he had been away during her mourning – yet it felt different now. Each day, she delighted in the colours of her clothes, rediscovering her wardrobe, and finding that some dresses were now so far out of fashion that they needed significant alteration.

Such things filled her time, but not her mind. Her heart and mind were focused, always and only, on Charles, on thoughts of what he might be doing, where he might be, when he might return. She found herself eager to hear of his travels, and of the progress of his improvements to Hunter's estates.

As January approached February, the snows slowed, and the first faint shoots of grass pushed through it, seeking warmth. Maria began to feel braver – she could not imagine hiding from the world forever. She allowed her mother to convince her to go into the closest town with her, and was pleased to discover that no one they met did more than greet her politely. Here, it was as if the scandals and accusations of Myniard House had never existed.

The relief was enormous.

Not long after, Maria was sitting in the parlour at Meltonbrook Chase, whilst Nerissa talked about gardens, and her plans for the future. Maria was still a little overwhelmed by the fact that Nerissa was increasing – a fact which she had shyly revealed a few weeks before. She was not sure how to feel – she was happy for Nerissa, but somehow sad – would she ever have a child of her own?

The thought brought a blush to her cheeks, for it made her think of Charles and her hopes for the future, and think of her time as Edmund's wife, and what happened in the marriage bed. The two thoughts together were enough to make her feel heated through, and flustered. She turned her attention back to Nerissa, and pushed those thoughts aside.

Moments later, the door opened. Maria looked up, startled to see Charles.

"Good day, Nerissa. Maria – I am glad you are here."

"Charles..." she looked at him, caught by how handsome he was, how well he looked. He came to her, and dropped to the couch beside her. Nerissa watched, a sparkle of amusement in her eyes.

"Maria..." for the first time, she noticed that he was carrying something. A small flat parcel. She looked at it curiously. "I... it's your birthday soon and I..."

He held out the parcel, and she took it, pleased, and uncertain at once. That he had remembered her birthday filled her with happiness. Gently, carefully, she unwrapped it, and lifted the lid on the delicately carved box. Inside lay a brooch, of the type designed for pinning on a bonnet or other headdress. It was silver, in the swirled shape of a bird with flowing feathers, each curve of it sparkling with green gems, and from it curved a small cluster of feathers – each a very dark green, yet glittering with a golden iridescence where the light caught them.

"It's beautiful, so very beautiful..."

He smiled at her, that smile that always made her melt completely.

"I have carried that for more than a year. I bought it last year when we were at Myniard House. I had intended to give it to you for your birthday, then, inappropriate as that might have been at the time – it just seemed so right for you. But then, before I could, the necklace and note from Edmund arrived. I could not, not after that. I put it aside, and vowed to wait. I made sure that, this year, I would be here for your birthday, and... this year, now, to give you a gift seemed more appropriate, more in tune with my hopes."

Tears rose in Maria's eyes, blurring the shining green gems of the brooch to a scattered emerald sparkle. He had carried it for a year, awaiting the time when he might give it to her. So long... She looked up into his concerned face, and leant forward, brushing a feather soft kiss to his lips before drawing back.

"Thank you. This means so much to me..."

He cupped her hands, where they held the brooch, and smiled, his face full of a happiness she shared. After a few moments, Nerissa cleared her throat, and they jumped a little, having been so caught up in each other that they had forgotten she was there.

"Would you care for some tea, Charles? And, if I can attract your attention away from my sister for a moment..." Nerissa's eyes sparkled with mischief as she spoke, "I have news – more things you've missed whilst away. I am increasing. You'll be an uncle later this year!"

Charles turned to her, his face filled with genuine delight.

"That's wonderful Nerissa! And is my mother driving you mad yet, with fussing?"

"Yes... and I am sure that it will just get more so from now on... unless of course, we find something else to distract her with..."

Nerissa looked significantly between Charles and Maria and waited. Maria flushed a bright red, but Charles laughed gently.

"You'll just have to wait and see what happens, won't you."

His tone of voice was as mischievous as Nerissa's and, suddenly, Maria felt light as air, and full of joy. It seemed that, even before they had allowed the world to see how they felt, their families had already come to their own conclusions, and were happy for them. It was a wonderful, wonderful day.

~~~~~

The distraction that Nerissa had hoped for came sooner than anyone expected, and from a different direction completely. When everyone from Meltonbrook Chase, except Charles (who had elected to stay behind, rather to Nerissa's continued amusement), left for London to attend the wedding of Miss Isabella Morton, the sister of another of the Hounds, Mr Raphael Morton, they had expected nothing more than a pleasant event and a meeting with friends.

By the time they returned, Charles' and Hunter's sister, Lady Alyse, was betrothed to Lord Tillingford, another of the Hounds, and the Dowager Duchess had another wedding to arrange. That very successfully fulfilled Nerissa's desire for distraction, and left everyone wondering what could happen next.

It had been, Maria thought, when informed of it all by her laughing sister, a year of weddings, while she had mourned.

~~~~

The weeks before Lady Alyse's wedding seemed to fly by, and Charles was frequently glad to escape Meltonbrook Chase and the whirlwind that was his mother, to spend far more peaceful time with Marla. They walked in the gardens as the beginning of spring brought the first leaves and the buds of flowers, they rode through the Park, always staying away from anywhere more public, and Maria became steadily more relaxed, happier and, to Charles, more beautiful.

"You look wonderful today. Is that a new riding habit?"

Maria blushed, and nodded.

"Yes, mother insisted. The local seamstress is far more talented than I expected – we have ordered me more new dresses too. It is wonderful to be able to choose rich colours and fabrics, and have no one disapprove of my choices."

They rode in silence for a few minutes, before Charles asked, cautious, yet needing desperately to know.

"Does this mean that you are more confident about being seen in public, that we might, perhaps, soon allow the world to know of our feelings?"

"I… I am not yet certain of that. I have been to the local towns with Mother, and all has gone well, but… I am not very brave…"

She looked away, flushed, and a little sad. Charles reached across and took her hand as they rode, squeezing her fingers gently.

"Will you come to Alyse's wedding? And, perhaps, dance? With me? I seem to remember that, some months ago, at another wedding, I promised you dancing, as soon as it might be possible."

Her eyes lit with delight at the thought of it, and hope surged in Charles' heart.

"Oh, yes, you did! And yes, I believe that I can do that – if I am to take that large a step back into being active in society, I can't think of a better place to do so, than on such a happy occasion, surrounded by friends. I very much look forward to dancing with you."

Her voice had become soft and wistful, as if she wished them already there, and her fingers had tightened on his as she spoke.

"I will be counting the days until I can hold you in my arms, openly, in a room full of people."

"And dancing is the only socially acceptable way to do that, isn't it?"

"It is. I will make certain that it's a waltz – I want to hold you as close as I possibly can... forever."

Her fingers closed on his again, and her eyes shone with such love that it left him dizzy. They rode on in silence, not needing words.

~~~~~

Lady Alyse's wedding to Lord Tillingford was beautiful, and Maria, after an initial nervousness, relaxed and enjoyed being out in society again.

She was beginning to believe that all of the fuss surrounding Edmund's death might actually be forgotten, overtaken by far more interesting new scandals in the minds of the gossips of the *ton*. She allowed herself to dance with a number of gentlemen, mostly family and friends well known to her, but the part of the day that she waited for was the moment of her dance with Charles.

As promised, he had ensured that it was a waltz. As he gathered her into his arms, she could not imagine a way in which the day might be more perfect. She lifted her face to his, their eyes met, and the music carried them away. It was as if the ballroom at Meltonbrook Chase was empty of everyone but them. She did not care who saw, and what gossip might come from the moment, all she cared for, in that instant, was the feel of Charles holding her.

What might have been minutes or hours later, the music drew to a close, and they drifted to a stop at the side of the room. Gently, Charles took her hand, and drew her out through the doors onto the terrace. The view across the Meltonbrook Chase gardens was beautiful, the moonlight glinting on the small lake in the distance, and the first flowers of spring filling the air with delicate scents.

They stood, completely alone, and a deep sense of peace settled on Maria. It felt so right, to be with this man. She looked at him, suddenly a little shy.

"I must admit that I am finding the fact that widows are allowed so much more freedom exhilarating. Only as a widow could I stand here with you, alone, and not be instantly the subject of utter scandal. They may talk a little, but not much."

Charles laughed softly, and she thought it a wonderful sound, one full of joy in living, and shared happiness.

"I am equally glad of that fact. I have never been prone to causing scandal, and I have no intention of starting now!"

"I am glad of that – I have had quite enough of scandal in my life. I hope for something far more peaceful and enjoyable from now on."

Charles paused, and she watched him, watched the play of emotion across his face, and waited, wondering what thoughts ran through his mind. He reached out, and cupped her cheek, his fingers gentle, caressing her skin. She shivered with pleasure, a shiver that ran through her entire body. It was a sensation no other man had ever induced in her, and she revelled in it.

"Maria... can you trust me to protect you, always? Are you willing, now, to let the world see how we feel – may I speak to your father, and formally court you?"

She paused, for, although his words filled her with complete joy, her fear was still there. Then, mentally shaking herself, she pushed the fear aside.

"Yes, I trust you, always and completely. I believe that I can face the world now, with you by my side. I know that I seem hesitant about everything, but the memory of standing in that town square, humiliated... it is hard to forget."

He leant forward, slowly, bringing his lips to hers, his hand still gentle upon her cheek, and kissed her as if she were the most precious thing on earth.

"I will speak to your father tomorrow."

Chapter Sixteen

"Good Day, Lord Chester. Might I have a word with you?"

"Of course, Wareham, do come into my study. Is there some problem with the boundaries of our estates that we need to address?"

Charles followed him down the hall and into the study.

"No, my Lord, nothing of that nature. I have a far more personal question to ask you."

"Oh?"

"My Lord, may I have your permission to court your daughter, Maria?"

Lord Chester released a bark of laughter, startling Charles, then smiled broadly.

"Wondered when you'd get to the point, my boy. Not that, technically, you really have to ask me. She's a widow, and as such, can make her own choices. But I thank you for the courtesy."

"I would do everything I can to ensure that propriety is served, my Lord – she has seen enough of scandal and gossip."

"True, very true. And that's only what I'd expect of you." He looked at Charles' expression and laughed again, "You'd like an answer, I see. Stop worrying – I heartily approve of you courting her. From the moment of that incident with the highwaymen, I've seen it – she's only happy when she's with you – the rest of the time, she's just waiting for the next time she'll see you. After the fiasco of her marriage to Lord Granville, I'd not deny her something that makes her happy."

"Thank you, my Lord. I will dedicate my life to making her happy. I've wanted to do so since I was a boy, and I'll not fail now that I have the chance. I was concerned that my lack of significant title would concern you…"

"Once, I might have worried, you're right, but I think I've learned my lesson – Granville seemed everything a girl could want – title, money, position – yet he made her life a misery. You'll do better, and you're not without funds, or good family connections to support you. And I'm very aware of your skills with the estates – you're no wastrel to gamble things away – she'll never have that sort of worry with you."

"Again, thank you my Lord, for your faith in me."

"Just live up to it. I have to ask – have you told your mother of your intentions yet? I suspect that she'll be planning weddings before you've even had a chance to ask Maria, if I know her."

Charles laughed, shaking his head, amused at Lord Chester's astute assessment of the Dowager Duchess.

"I haven't – for exactly that reason. She'll work it out soon enough!"

"Very good then."

They spoke for a little longer, about estates, and about Charles' plans and hopes for the future, before Charles took his leave of Lord Chester, and went in search of Maria. He found her, as so often, curled on a couch in the parlour, reading. She looked up as he entered, and smiled. She was so beautiful that it took his breath away – he was the luckiest man imaginable!

He went to her, and dropped onto the seat beside her, taking her hands in his. The book slipped unregarded to the floor.

"I just spoke to your father. He approves of me courting you – he even said that he'd wondered when I would ask!"

"Oh! Well... that is good, I think – I would not want him to be unhappy about us, although... even if he was unhappy, I suspect that I might, for you, be brave enough to defy him."

He lifted her hand, and turned it over, pressing a kiss to her palm. Her scent surrounded him, and his mind was filled with the possibilities of a future with her by his side.

"Shall we celebrate? Will you allow me to drive you into the town, to take tea at that new little teashop?"

"What – right now?"

"Yes – why not? It is a rather beautiful day, almost beginning to feel truly like spring!"

She looked flustered for a moment, then nodded decisively.

"Yes, just let me change."

She rushed from the room with the energy and appetite for life that had delighted him when she was younger. It was so good to see her like that again. He lifted the fallen book from the floor, and placed it on the table, then stood to gaze out of the window while he waited.

~~~~~

The teashop was crowded, as people from the surrounding areas came to try the new offerings in the town, and Maria almost wanted to run away, there were so many people, so many she did not know. But with her hand on Charles' arm, she took a deep steadying breath, and continued.

The tea was delicious – a blend she had never tried before - and the little cakes served with it were both beautiful to see and delicately flavoured, with lemon, and exotic vanilla. She sat, and allowed the sounds to flow around her, hearing snippets of others' conversations – none of which were about her. Her confidence grew, and soon she was completely ignoring the people around them, and simply talking to Charles.

As always lately, their discussion was about his plans for woollen mills in the north, and about the successes of the new farming methods he had introduced on many of the estates. She found herself genuinely interested, and realised, with a start, that she had learned a great deal about business and farming, just from the conversations of the last year. What might she do with that knowledge? She did not know, but she would, she suspected, find out as the next few months went forward.

On the way back, as they sat close beside each other on the seat of his curricle, she finally felt brave enough to ask a question that had long preyed on her mind.

"Charles... what will your mother think of you courting me? My experience with the Dowager Countess has made me rather wary of..."

"Never fear, Maria – you've known my mother all your life, haven't you? You know that, no matter how imposing and autocratic she tries to seem, she always cares more for people's happiness than anything else. Especially since Father and Richard died in the accident. But I have no intention of mentioning it to her yet – I don't want her pushing us..."

Maria released a sigh of relief.

"Thank you! I do like your mother, but I think that if she made any attempt to direct me, I would be rather rude in response. After the Dowager Countess, I am resolved to never allow someone else to control me like that again."

"Perhaps a shock like that would not be a bad thing for my mother... but she does mean well, always."

"I will trust you to protect me from her enthusiasm. Or should I, more correctly, be trusting you to protect her from my prickliness?"

"Either will do – I will do my best to keep everyone happy – but you most of all."

Maria nodded, and let the conversation lapse, instead admiring the way he handled the horses, and enjoying the early spring sun, savouring the fact that she had been brave, had been seen in public with Charles, and that nothing bad had happened.

~~~~~

"Do have another cake, Lady Chester."

"I simply couldn't, Your Grace, delicious as they are."

The Dowager Duchess smiled at her neighbours, wondering about the cause of their visit. Not that they were distant neighbours in any way, but this visit seemed out of the normal run of things. She was sure that there was a purpose behind it.

"Aaah… Your Grace, there is a reason for our call today – beyond the excellence of your hospitality."

"I suspected as much, Lord Chester – please do explain."

"It's about our daughter – and your son," at the Duchess' concerned expression, Lord Chester went on hastily, "no, no, not Hunter and Nerissa. Charles and Maria. Charles has asked my permission to court Maria, and I have given it."

"That's wonderful! I did see the indications that things were moving that way, but I was rather distracted by Alyse's wedding. Do you expect that we'll have another wedding to plan? I do so love organising weddings!"

"I suspect that we will. But… I wanted to ask your forbearance. Maria is still very shy of society, and public visibility, after her unpleasant experiences at Myniard House. The Dowager Countess is a most unpleasant woman, who tried her hardest to control Maria's every movement, and to make her life miserable. Maria is, I believe, terrified of ever being in such a position again. I would not want your enthusiasm to be misinterpreted as being overbearing."

The Dowager Duchess considered for a moment, deciding whether to be offended or not. In the end, if she was wholly honest with herself, she could understand Lord Chester's fear. She knew that she was enthusiastic, and sometimes domineering, to a fault. She took a deep breath, and told herself to be gracious.

"I see. Thank you for the warning. I am, I know, a little overwhelming at times, to those who do not know me as well. My own children cheerfully defy me, to my chagrin, yet all has worked out well for them, in general. Am I correct in the understanding that you are asking me to politely ignore Charles and Maria's affection for each other, until such time as they tell me themselves?"

"Yes, Your Grace, that is exactly what I am hoping you will do. I believe that they will be far happier if left to come to things in their own time – and I must say that I do not expect it to take very long."

"I will, as you ask, pretend not to see. But I will start planning a wedding anyway, with your connivance, if you will – I do so enjoy it, and this is the last of my children to marry…"

"Of course. I think that we might all enjoy a little discreet planning."

"We are agreed then."

They went back to the tea and cakes, all well pleased with their agreement.

~~~~~

April went by in a haze of increasingly beautiful spring days and Charles delayed leaving on his usual rounds of Hunter's estates. He could not bear to leave Maria – she was more beautiful every day, more confident and happy. They drove or rode out most days, no longer afraid to be seen together, allowing the world to see them.

He had expected, by now, to have been questioned by his mother, for the Dowager Duchess simply could not be unaware of his actions, but she was uncharacteristically silent. He was grateful, if puzzled.

The more time he spent with Maria, the more days that went by without anything but happiness, the less he wanted to wait – it was time to ask her the final question. They had spoken of the future, of his plans, of the things that she would like to do, but they had, always, avoided the word 'marriage' – he had to assume that was because it still echoed in her mind attached to her miserable year at Myniard House. It was time to change that, it was time for him to ask her to marry him – but where, and when?

~~~~~

It was May, and Maria could hardly believe how different her life was, now. Each day that she spent with Charles was wonderful, but she had reached the point where she wanted more. Would he ask her to marry him? She did not know. She wanted him to, oh how much she wanted that. Her patience was wearing thin. At least she had a distraction. Nerissa and Hunter had not gone to London for the Season, due to Nerissa being increasing, so Nerissa had decided to hold a Ball.

It might not be as glittering as those in London, but Meltonbrook Chase would host a sizeable crowd of the nobility, and everyone was looking forward to the entertainment. Even Maria, who had been recruited to assist with the arrangements.

On the night of the Ball, Maria stood before the mirror, staring at her reflection. She barely recognised herself. Annie had worked wonders with her hair, which was piled high and featured a tiny headpiece, attached to which was the beautiful brooch and feathers that Charles had given her. The dress she wore echoed the colours of the feathers – a pale green underlayer, overlaid with a fine dark net, which was covered in hundreds of tiny glittering beads, as iridescent as the feathers. It was a stunning piece of work, and she adored it. She hoped that Charles would love it too – the thought of seeing him made her warm all over, as it always did.

She descended the stairs, and the carriage took them to Meltonbrook Chase. She felt as if the last two years had never happened, as if she was a young girl in her first season, all over again, giddy with excitement and longing. It was, she decided, a far nicer sensation the second time around.

When they entered the foyer, where Charles stood with the rest of his family, receiving the guests, her eyes went straight to him. He finished greeting Lady Willforth, and turned. She knew the instant that he saw her, for he stilled utterly, his eyes widening. Then he smiled, the smile that made him seem even more handsome than usual, the smile that made her forget that anyone else existed, and he held out his hand. She took it.

"I did not think it possible that you could look more beautiful than ever before, but you do. That gown is magnificent."

"It is, isn't it?"

Nerissa's voice contained envy, and she sighed in awe of the gown, which Maria had intentionally not shown her before.

"Thank you! But I should move on into the ballroom, I am holding up your receiving line."

Charles released her hand, reluctantly, and Maria moved past him, and away. Suddenly the time until he would be finished greeting guests seemed interminable, she wished, with such intensity, that he was by her side.

But the time passed, as time does, no matter how we wish to speed or slow it, and finally, as she stood with her parents at one side of the room, he appeared before her. He bowed over her hand, his eyes sparkling with something that might have been mischief.

"Will you grant me the delight of dancing with you, my Lady?"

"I will, my Lord."

He offered her his arm, and led her away. Unseen by Maria, her parents exchanged a satisfied look as she left them. They joined the set for that was forming for the dance, and soon Maria was laughing, enjoying the simple pleasure of the bouncing country dance, the steps coming back to her, even after so long unpractised. By the time the music ended, she was short of breath, and overheated. Charles offered his arm, and they moved to the refreshment table then, glasses in hand, they settled on a couch at one side of the room, in a quieter corner.

"It is wonderful to see you laughing and enjoying yourself. You were so subdued for far too long."

"I was, wasn't I? I did not realise how much life at Myniard house changed me, until now. Tonight, I feel as if, finally, I have left all of that behind."

Charles looked at her, his eyes filled with love, and she wanted, immediately, to melt against him, to feel his arms around her. She did not move, but her expression must have made her thoughts clear.

"Walk with me? On the terrace?"

"Yes."

Her voice came soft, a little shaky as she rose. She felt as if something momentous was about to happen, as if the evening was a fairytale, filled with magic. He led her to the terrace, and along to the far end, where tiny climbing roses were blooming in a sprawl over the balustrade and the wall of the house. The scent was intoxicating. They stood, and time slowed, the only sound the hard beating of her heart. She watched as he raised his arms and reached for her, and went into his arms willingly. The scent of the roses was joined by the even more intoxicating scent of him.

He tilted her face up, and their eyes met. When his lips brushed hers, her eyes fluttered shut, and she gave herself entirely to the sensation. No memories of the past tarnished the moment. There was only Charles, only now, only happiness.

When he finally drew back a little, she opened her eyes, feeling the loss of his lips on hers as an almost physical pain.

"Maria, my darling Maria, I have waited long enough, I think, we both have. Maria, will you marry me? I cannot imagine life without you, could not bear to live in such emptiness."

Her heart beat faster, her breath hitched, and her mouth felt dry. He had said the words – the words that she had wanted to hear for so long now. She rose onto her toes, and brought her lips to touch his, butterfly soft.

"Yes," she whispered against his lips, then the world swirled away as his arms tightened around her, and he deepened the kiss, filling it with all of the longing for her that he had carried for so many years.

When they went back into the ballroom, they went straight to where her parents stood, talking to Charles' mother.

"I wish to inform you that Lady Granville has just done me the honour of agreeing to become my wife."

Almost before the words were out of his mouth, the Dowager Duchess was speaking.

"At last! I thought that you would never get to it. I do so love weddings!"

Everyone laughed, and, as the Dowager Duchess and Lady Chester turned to each other, and instantly began discussing wedding plans, Charles drew Maria away, and swept her into his arms, and out to dance the waltz that was just beginning.

Epilogue

In the end, Maria's only request for the wedding was that it be as different as possible from her first wedding. So, instead of St George's in London, it was held at the church in Meltonbrook village, and the guest list was relatively small, although the extended group of friends and family was still quite large. The dress that Maria wore was simple, yet more beautiful for it. It was a shimmering gold lace over a rich cream underskirt, and embellished with tiny red gems scattered over the lace. In the summer sun that June, the dress, and her golden hair, caught the light, and she seemed to glow, like an angel, or something magical.

Charles watched, enraptured, as she walked towards him. Every time he thought that she could not look more beautiful, she did so. That she was finally to be his seemed unreal, yet it was true. She reached his side, and the ceremony began – passing in a blur of happiness, where he was, in every instant, utterly aware of Maria, beside him. Finally, the last words were spoken, and they turned to step out of the church.

The sunlight through the small stained-glass windows cast shards of colour over them as they moved, and time seemed slowed. They stepped through the door, and, as Charles had expected, were greeted by a veritable cascade of rose petals. He pulled her into his arms, there on the steps, in front of everyone, and kissed her.

~~~~~

Maria woke slowly, cocooned in warmth. She opened her eyes, and memory came rushing back. She was married again! She turned to watch Charles, as the morning light through the window cast his handsome face into sharp relief. This was how she wanted to wake every morning – in the arms of the man she loved.

Tomorrow, they would leave here, leave Chester Park and Meltonbrook Chase behind, and travel north. As a wedding present, Hunter had gifted them Millford Grange, the estate that Charles had long wanted to use as the start of a business in woollen mills.

Maria could not imagine a better life than the one before her – a far cry from the bright social swirl that she had imagined herself living, before she had married Edmund. Now, whilst some Seasons in London would be enjoyable, she looked forward to long years with Charles, mostly spent on their estate.

And, best of all, she was no longer Lady Granville. Now, she was Viscountess Wareham. Lady Wareham was a far more appealing name, far more. Now, there was nothing, absolutely nothing, left of that terrible year to taint her life.

Even her memories of the marital bed had been replaced. She looked at Charles, her lips curving into a happy smile. Now, she finally understood what Nerissa had meant, all those months ago in London.

"You look happy, my darling."

"I am, I am so very happy, husband."

He pulled her to him, and kissed her, and everything else became irrelevant. There was time – she had the rest of her life to build with him.

The End.

About the Author

Arietta Richmond has been a compulsive reader and writer all her life. Whilst her reading has covered an enormous range of topics, history has always fascinated her, and historical novels have been amongst her favourite reading.

She has written a wide range of work, from business articles and other non-fiction works (published under a pen name) but fiction has always been a major part of her life. Now, her Regency Historical Romance books are finally being released. The Derbyshire Set is comprised of 10 novels (7 released so far). The 'His Majesty's Hounds' series is comprised of 16 novels, with the thirteenth having just been released.

She also has a standalone longer novel shortly to be released, and two other series of novels in development.

She lives in Australia, and when not reading or writing, likes to travel, and to see in person the places where history happened.

Be the first to know about it when Arietta's next book is released!

Sign up to Arietta's newsletter at

http://www.ariettarichmond.com

When you do, you will receive two free subscriber exclusive books - **'A Gift of Love'**, which is a prequel to the Derbyshire Set series, and ends on the day that 'The Earl's Unexpected Bride' begins, and **'Madame's Christmas Marquis'** which is an additional story in the His Majesty's Hounds series

These stories are not for sale anywhere – they are absolutely exclusive to newsletter subscribers!

Here is your preview of

Betting on a Lady's Heart

His Majesty's Hounds – Book 14
Sweet and Clean Regency Romance

Arietta Richmond

Chapter One

Gervaise Belmont, Viscount Woodridge, was a man who had once had it all, then almost lost it. And he was at risk of losing it all again.

He was young still, only twenty-four, and handsome, his jaw strong and square, his hair dark, with reddish glints amongst its strands. His eyes were the green of spring leaves in the sun, and his smile was warm and brought a dimple to both cheeks. Women loved him, and indeed, he enjoyed them likewise, although he had yet to find one he thought he could care for enough to marry. His father had been lucky enough to find love in two marriages, and with that example before him, he was loath to consider accepting less.

But there was one thing that drew Gervaise more than women. The races. Horses, frantic as they jockeyed for position, the men atop their backs looking as though they would fall underneath their steed at any moment, the large hooves breaking them into pieces.

Gervaise's family had never lacked for money, unlike many titled families, but it had a way of finding its way out of his pocket and into the possession of others. He gambled as easily as most men breathed. Cards, dice, any number of other passions, but the horses, that was the largest offender. He had, after his unpleasant adventures of the previous year, sworn off serious gambling – but that was a hard promise to keep. The lure of the excitement was strong, and he struggled. Today, he had promised himself that he would enjoy the races, and only bet a tiny amount, just to reduce the craving for gambling.

He made his way to the bookmaker and smiled.

"Back again my Lord?" the man asked.

"Indeed. Although I'll not be wagering large amounts today."

The old man looked at him, his expression cynical, and laughed. He had wiry white hair and had to squint when he read anything, which had left him with an array of wrinkles around his eyes.

"Which race?" he asked.

Gervaise told him, the bookmaker quoted the odds, and Gervaise chose which horse to bet on, then passed a purse full of coins to the man.

The bookmaker took the bag and whistled.

"This would feed my family for years to come," he remarked.

Gervaise hesitated a moment, his thoughts going back to the poor woodcutters who had saved his life a year past. They would have said the same. It was hard to reconcile the way that money existed in his life, with the way it existed in the lives of the common people.

He shrugged the thoughts aside, and focussed on his purpose. He needed the thrill of the bet, of watching the race, to hold him through the next weeks and months of not gambling.

"Perhaps you should occasionally have a bet yourself – one win could change your life," Gervaise said, smiling as he did so. The booking agent laughed, and wrote up a slip for Gervaise to take with him.

"Not likely, my Lord, for one loss could send us to the poorhouse. I'm a father with children to feed, after all, so I'll not be risking it – I'll leave that to the likes of you, who can afford the losses," the man nodded to Gervaise.

The man's words brought Gervaise's own father to mind, and he sighed as he turned away.

Gervaise's father was Nicholas Belmont, the Earl of Amberhithe, a man who had been remarkably patient with his son, at a time when they both grieved the death of Gervaise's mother.

During that terrible few years was when Gervaise had developed his love of gambling – it had seemed a harmless distraction from his grief, but it was a distraction that had cost him all of his funds, and nearly his life. A wise investment after one big win had saved his funds, but almost too late for his life. He still walked with a slight limp today, as a result of his foolishness. He never wanted to be in such a desperate situation again.

Gervaise's mind was keen and sharp, though the intricacies of good finance had been lost on him for most of his life.

He had, in recent times, been trying to remedy that, but the lure of gambling still drew him, even though he knew, now, that it would never be a wise activity, financially. Hence the visit to the racetrack today.

The place was called Green Hill, and indeed the backdrop of the track, the side opposite the stands, was a green hill, which rose upwards at a sharp angle before levelling out.

The track was a rather wondrous place, where the human dregs of London mixed with the Lords that made up high society. Men of high standing wore fine top hats which may cost many times more than the whole outfit of the man who stood next to them at the fence, cheering their respective horses on.

Gervaise was comfortable amongst the mixed crowd, having always got on well with those of lesser standing, coming from a family who appreciated their servants and farmers well. His experience of a year past had increased his appreciation for the innate humanity of people of all stations in life, for it had been a family of poor woodcutters who had saved his life.

It was his charm and his wit which drew people to him, man or woman, and he was glad of it, never having been a man for a solitary existence.

It began to rain as he stood at the edge of the stands, bracing himself against the fence. He had put a considerable part of the funds he'd brought on one horse, a grey beast that stood out among the black and bay colors of the other horses. The race began, the stallions throwing up mud as they ran. Around Gervaise the crowd was deafening, as men and women alike supported their favoured horses loudly.

The familiar excitement coursed through him, the sense of everything hanging on the thin thread of chance, and he felt his heart beat faster, the world around him suddenly seeming cast in sharp relief, every detail precise and vibrant.

The grey horse won, by a large margin, much to Gervaise's delight. His considerable winnings would certainly ensure that he did not need to dip into the funds he had invested, and he would be able to set a few affairs in order, without disappointing his father by depleting those investments. He hurried to collect his winnings.

But the little voice in the back of his mind whispered as he did so – *'see, a good win – you could do that again, and again, and again….'*.

Chapter Two

Clarisse Weston groaned as her step mother Helena threw open the window covering, allowing the bright light of morning into her bedchamber.

"Surely it is not yet time to get up," Clarisse said as she squeezed her eyes shut.

"It is indeed," Helena said sharply, her eyes narrowing at her step daughter. "Your father may allow you to sleep half the day away, but now that I am here, you shall not."

Clarisse's father was Arthur Weston, heir to the Weston fortune, which had been made throughout the years by her father's, and before him his father's, astute business dealings. Her mother had died giving birth to her, leaving her an only child.

Other women came and went in her father's life, but only for short moments. It had seemed that it would just be Clarisse and her father, as close as two peas in a pod, at least until she married, which she supposed she eventually would.

And then Helena had come into their lives, her features soft and pretty, her frame lithe and slim. She was far younger than Arthur, but significantly older than Clarisse. She had captured Arthur's heart, though she had done little to endear herself to Clarisse. The younger woman was sure that her new stepmother was more attracted to her father's money than she was to his person – but she knew that her father would not believe that, he was far too enamoured of Helena.

Clarisse rolled out of bed and Helena left her. Abby, her maid, hurried in and helped her to dress. When she made her way downstairs shortly after, she found her father in the breakfast room, smoking a cigar as he perused a newspaper, his breakfast on the plate before him.

"Father," she said, kissing him on the cheek.

He folded his paper and set it aside as he smiled. When she said nothing more, he shook his head a little.

"I thought you would chastise me for having a cigar so early in the morning"

He was barrel chested and strong, with dark hair, a bushy greying moustache, and grey eyes. His daughter was slim, with delicate pale skin, and soft brown hair. Her eyes were hazel, and took on more green when she was outside, or by the window. She took a seat opposite her father. They often ate together in the breakfast room, and Helena rarely, if ever, joined them, preferring to take her morning meal in her own rooms.

"I would normally, but I understand why you might need such a soothing vice of late."

Her father shook his head and held his hand up.

"If this is to be another attack on my wife…"

"No, nothing of the sort."

She was eighteen years old, and her father had spoiled her. Whatever she had wanted he had provided for her, but her personality was such that she had never abused her father's willingness to shower her with gifts. They had survived together in what she had thought was utter bliss. The fact that he had married Helena suggested that he had not been of the same opinion. That thought hurt.

It was not as though her father had begun treating her differently since he had married, it was simply that Helena seemed determined to overstep her bounds. An eighteen-year-old girl who had done without a mother did not suddenly need one, in Clarisse's opinion. Helena felt differently. She seemed intent on providing rules and structure, where none was needed, or at least wanted.

"When will you and Helena have your own children?"

"Do not start that," her father chuckled as he extinguished his cigar and pulled his plate before him. "I am too old."

"Helena is not." Clarisse's tone was tart. She always reminded her father that his new wife was rather apart from him in age.

"I wonder if, just once, you would not tease me," Arthur said with a barking laugh.

"Perhaps, but if so, it will not be today."

Clarisse grinned, and they ate in silence, until her father pushed his plate away, finished and, looked at Clarisse, meeting her eyes squarely.

"I know that you do not like her. I know you would never speak so plainly, but I know it."

Clarisse sighed, and opened her mouth to speak, but found herself unable to honestly refute her father's words, so closed her mouth and waited for the man to say more.

"Though you never met your mother, I know that there must be some sort of... loyalty you feel towards her. Believe me, I do understand - it's that same loyalty that I carried which kept me from marrying again for so long."

Clarisse nodded. Her father was right of course, as he so often was. Though she hadn't known her mother, she had still been her mother, and her father moving on, even after eighteen years, seemed like a betrayal to her, though she knew that most men remarried far sooner. Helena had, from the start, irritated Clarisse, and the idea of letting her into Clarisse's good graces and confidence had felt as if it would also be a betrayal. So she had built a wall up between her and the older woman, unwilling to allow any kind of friendly interaction. Her stepmother's irritating attitudes had made that somewhat simpler to do, as well.

"I loved your mother," Arthur went on to his daughter. "She was a light so bright in my already bright life that she made it seem that much duller when she was out of it. I'm a blessed man. My family made a name for itself long before I had to do any real work. I've simply steered the ship from crashing into the rocks near the shore, and reaped the reward. I met your mother, a beautiful woman who blessed me with you, who somehow filled me with even more love than she did. Losing your mother was the worst thing that had ever happened to me, I have no doubt that you will believe that."

He paused a moment, watching her, then went on.

"Even though all around me told me that I should remarry, that I should get myself a son who could inherit the business, for so very long, I simply couldn't bear the thought. Until Helena."

Clarisse felt hot tears sting her eyes, and she dabbed at them with the corner of her napkin. She thought of her mother often, and had through the years, having to settle upon an imaginary representation of the woman she had never actually known. In her mind her mother had been kind and loving and full of life. Her father had spoken of her often, and she had built up her image of the woman from that. And then she had been replaced. It hadn't been sudden, it had taken a long time, but still, it felt as though her mother had lost her place in her father's heart. No matter how many times he assured her that had not happened.

"Helena woke me up this morning, again," Clarisse said, when her father had fallen quiet, apparently considering his explanation of his marriage over.

"How horrid," her father remarked dryly.

"She makes me tighten my stays. I can barely breathe."

"She wants you to look feminine."

Clarisse laughed.

"I'm a woman. I can't get much more feminine, father."

"You actively misunderstand me," her father scowled. "Helena has your best interests at heart, if you can believe that." Clarisse narrowed her eyes, but she did not speak. Arthur went on. "She wishes for you to find a man, to marry well."

"I have a man. My father. The best man I know."

She could see the pride shine in her father's eyes, but he shook his head gently and waved his hand at her.

"You cannot marry your father my dear," he said.

"I'm only eighteen."

"More than one girl has been married at seventeen or eighteen," her father warned.

"I am willing to consider marrying. Just don't let her have a say in it."

Her father scoffed audibly.

"I tire of having this conversation, over and over."

Clarisse knew that the discussion was over, that nothing useful would be gained by persisting. Sighing, she stood and left the table.

Continued...

Get

"Betting on a Lady's Heart"

as soon as it's released – go to
http://www.ariettarichmond.com

and make sure that you are signed up for news and release notices!

ARIETTA RICHMOND

Books in the 'His Majesty's Hounds' Series

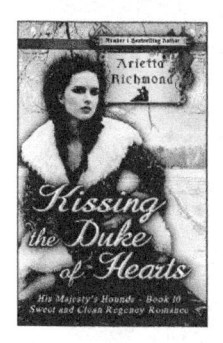

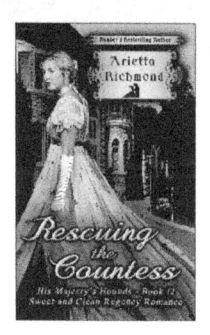

Attracting the Spymaster (coming soon)
Restoring the Earl's Honour (coming soon)

Books in 'The Derbyshire Set'

The Earl's Unexpected Bride

The Captain's Compromised Heiress

The Viscount's Unsuitable Affair

The Count's Impetuous Seduction

The Rake's Unlikely Redemption

The Marquess' Scandalous Mistress

The Marchioness' Second Chance (**Coming Soon!**)

Lady Theodora's Christmas Wish

The Derbyshire Set Omnibus Edition Vol. 1 (the first three books all in one)

The Derbyshire Set Omnibus Edition Vol. 2 (the second three books all in one)

Available at all good book stores and for ebook readers too!

ARIETTA RICHMOND

Regency Collections with Other Authors

Love, a Duke at Christmas
The Duke's Secret
The Duke's Christmas Bride
Kissing the Duke of Hearts

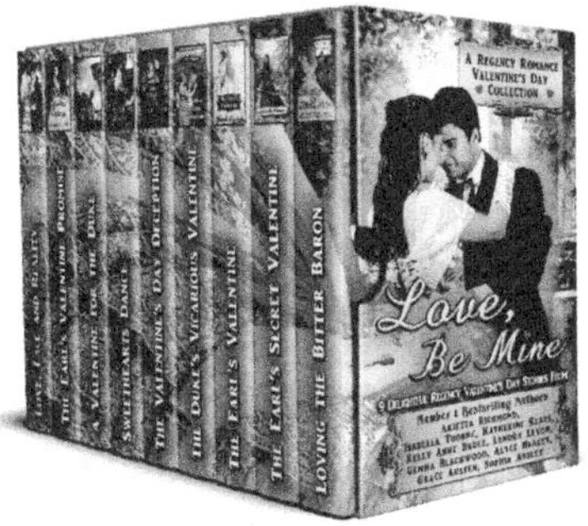
A Regency Romance Valentine's Day Collection
Love, Be Mine
The Earl's Valentine
The Earl's Secret Valentine
Loving the Bitter Baron

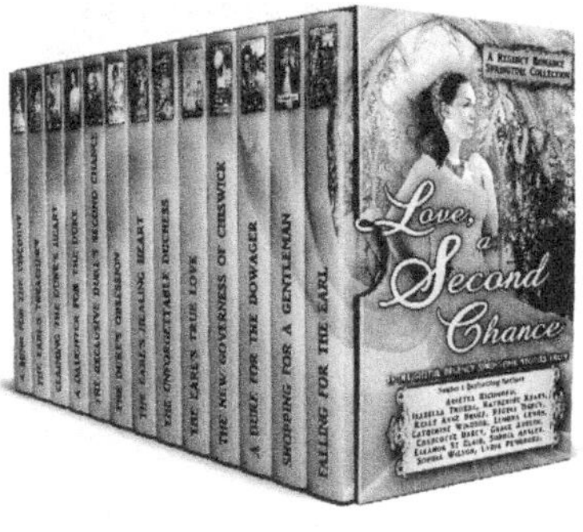
Love, a Second Chance
A Bride for the Dowager
Shopping for a Gentleman
Falling for the Earl

Other Books from Dreamstone Publishing

Dreamstone publishes books in a wide variety of categories, ranging from Erotica and Romance to Kids Books, Books on Writing, Business Books, Photography, Cook Books, Diaries, Coloring books and much more. New books are released each month.

Be the first to know when our next books are coming out

Be first to get all the news – sign up for our newsletter at

http://www.dreamstonepublishing.com

Made in the USA
Monee, IL
30 July 2022